BORDER SHOCK

Morgan Winfeld in New York

By Pam Robertson

Border Shock
Morgan Winfeld in New York

by Pam Robertson

Any errors in this text are strictly the responsibility of the author, who not only ignores the inconvenience of certain impossibilities out in the real world, but as a writer, takes true joy in making things up.

ISBN: 978-1-9995004-2-9 (digital version)
        978-0-9995004-1-2 (print version)

Cover design for the original book in this series by Letsgetbooked.com
Cover design for this book by Pam Robertson

Dedication

This book is for the ones we've lost
The brothers and dads
The moms and sisters
The family and friends whose
loss is felt on special days
and run of the mill days
Rest until we
can start the shenanigans all over.

A   N o t e   o n   T i m e

    Since Morgan is a spy working within an agency and alongside police, FBI, military, and paramilitary groups, the times referred to in the working scenes of this book reflect a 24 hour clock. This makes the story read as legit, but I don't want to leave a reader in the dark, so I thought an explanation might be helpful here.

    If you have trouble sorting out the 24 hour clock, may I suggest you play with it a bit. Set your phone, watch, and bedside alarm on a 24 hour clock while you enjoy the book. Have fun with it!

Here's a cheat sheet on the 24 hour clock:
    Morning hours are preceded by zero.
    0600 (pronounced oh-six hundred or oh-six hundred hours) is 6:00 a.m.
    0930 hrs (pronounced oh-nine-thirty) is 9:30 a.m.
    Time that occurs in the afternoon or evening, you simply add twelve
    1300 hrs is 1:00 p.m.
    1600 hrs is 4:00 p.m.
    1615 is 4:15 p.m.
    For midnight, it's best to avoid confusion by using 2359 or 0001 and then everyone shows up on the correct day.

Chapter One
New York, NY

Morgan sipped her coffee and looked over at the FBI agent. The American government had been very clear they didn't want international help, and it had taken ages to get them involved in global efforts to fight cyber crime. Morgan had made a friendly visit to the FBI and CIA head offices during a visit at American Thanksgiving, and helped pave the way for this level of cooperation to get started. She and Skelter, the agent assigned to work with her, were trying to make some fast headway.

On this dreary morning, Morgan wasn't enjoying much as she sat in the cinder block room. He was a fine agent; he'd been recognized for being effective, organized, and the wrong person to be pitted against in a fist fight. He'd been a wrestler in his teens, and became an avid fan and then a student of mixed marital arts so he knew how to handle himself in a fight. Skelter's dark hair was greying at the temples, and he was slender and tall. He dressed more casually than a lot of his counterparts, but looked good in his deliberately faded denim and the open collared dress shirts with sleeves rolled up two turns. He was struggling with today's assignment, and she was okay making him squirm a bit.

Skelter looked over at Morgan just as she looked away. "You're staring at me again," he said.

"I can't help it. And I don't mean to, but sometimes you make it hard not to. You're a fine looking specimen of a man." She paused for dramatic effect and shrugged. "Sorry."

"I don't think you're sorry at all. You see me as a piece of meat," he whined.

"I do not! I respect the me too movement, and everything it stands for," she said adamantly. She made a hashtag with her fingers to prove her point.

"I call bullshit," he expounded.

Morgan sighed as she placed her elbow on the table, and then rested her head in her upturned hand. "We suck at this," she said.

"We do?" Skelter said, his voice back to his usual deep tones. "I thought that was better than the last three times."

"No, we officially suck at role play. If I was listening in on this conversation, I'd want to stab myself in the eye."

"How good does it have to be? We just need to record a few lines that're long enough to have the cyber stalkers start honing in on you."

Morgan smiled crookedly, and let out an exasperated sigh for dramatic effect. "Skelter, we are practicing a few lines but need to stretch this into a five minute conversation. And we might need a dozen of these conversations plus text exchanges for the cyber trolls to find me and turn their focus this way."

"Ugh," he said, rubbing his hand across his eyes while reaching for a coffee cup. He was standing at the edge of the room, and his body cast long shadows in the yellow light. "There must be a better way, but I'm feeling distracted. We were up twice with our youngest last night, and I'm beat."

"Why didn't you say so? We can do this later," Morgan said. She tried to sympathize with Skelter, who was an older dad to youngsters, something that was not easily accomplished with the rigours that his job demanded. It wasn't something she completely understood, not having children of her own, but she tried to be empathetic. Besides, she needed Skelter's cooperation and full attention to get this done and though they had already been working this case together for several weeks, there was no need to finish it all today. Morgan was willing to adapt their plans to keep him engaged.

Morgan's employer, the Agency for Crime and Terror Interception – or ACTI – had been approached by members of EU and Interpol to do something about the skyrocketing occurrences of cyber crime. This mission was an international effort.

"Let's try it again," Skelter said. "Just ask my wife and she'll vouch for me. I can break a woman's heart without it seeming all that difficult. We'll get these guys to buy in to what we are doing."

"Ha! No doubt in my mind at all, Skelter," Morgan laughed. She didn't laugh much, but when she did her eyes lit up. Her dark hair was a short mess of waves that were being encouraged by the humidity, sculpted with gel to keep it all under control. She enjoyed life better when things were under control.

Convincing the United States president that an international agency like ACTI, along with FBI and police forces in the U.S., could do something about cyber crime had not been an easy task. The president wanted Interpol to look after the problem, and it took some heavy handed educating before he understood that Interpol didn't have officers on the ground like they show in the movies. Interpol was an international agency that coordinated police activity, but it was ACTI – a term President Trump had not heard before – who would do the work along with American federal agents and local police forces in this case.

Morgan was familiar with persuasion tactics, and she knew this particular president needed to be absolutely certain they would get results before he would commit. She had leveraged the skill of her team and her position as the Assistant Director of Field Operations so that the president's wife started getting hounded regularly by email and text messages. Once the first lady discovered she couldn't opt out or block the messages herself, she pushed the president to take action on cyber crime. Morgan was grateful to her cousin, James, at ACTI, since he was the one who'd been able to make the cyber stalking against the first lady appear legitimate. James was an exceptional technical agent with outstanding computer skills, and his stealthy work finally ended six months of pressure from the international community when the president signed on.

Morgan and Skelter started working together in early November. As an international agency most members of the public didn't know ACTI existed. Few countries who contributed to it knew what ACTI stood for, but governments around the world knew who to call when they needed covert operations, including good old fashioned spy work combined with cutting edge technology.

In the six weeks since she started working with Skelter, he had shown strong leadership through the sad and sometimes destitute circumstances they found. Victims of cyber crime were typically women in their fifties to seventies. They often lived alone, many were either widowed or divorced, and some of them were financially ruined by the time they – or someone in their family – figured out what was happening.

Morgan was still trying to determine how the cyber stalkers found their targets, aside from the random success with an algorithm or robocalls. Many of the victims weren't active on social media, others got haunted by untraceable email. Victims banked with different institutions, lived in different cities, and had no connections to each other that could be identified. Although obituaries were considered a good source of information for stalkers at one time, there were far less of them being published nowadays.

Skelter had a good track record for solving cases and cleaning up the mess that organized crime created in the U.S. His wife worked as a paramedic, and they had two young kids who were being raised with the help of a rotating fleet of nannies.

"Something's not right," Skelter said after they had given up on making more recordings for the day. He rubbed the fatigue from his stubble covered chin. He was looking at a secure computer terminal, waiting to see what the morning internet chatter looked like. "These folks we are watching have been talking consistently for the past six weeks and normally don't sleep. Right now, things are all quiet except for talk of some kind of problem here in Manhattan. What gives?"

"Do you want me to contact James at the ACTI office and get him to look around for some more traffic?" Morgan asked. "He's analyzing data from big networks, including some shadowy, dark web ones."

Before Skelter finished answering her, a police officer opened the door with a thud. The arm at the top of the door, meant to assist in opening and closing, dangled uselessly at the fierceness of the push.

"Look, I know you guys are here for other purposes, but the shift commander is asking you to come to a briefing. We've got big problems." The officer's voice was shaking. *Nerves, or fear?* Morgan wondered. He was in his mid-forties, roughly the same age as Morgan and Skelter. They quickly followed him down a short corridor toward the glass-walled briefing room as he introduced himself. "I'm Sergeant Ricky Miles. Commander Richards is about to put out one hell of a call for support, and he asked me to include you both."

"Thanks for coming," Commander Richards said, nodding toward Morgan and Skelter as they found a place to stand along the back wall. The commander looked over each person in the room of thirty officers. He smoothed back his grey hair as if he was readying his head for his police hat, cleared his throat loudly, then slurped from a paper coffee cup.

"We've got a problem," he said, clearing his throat again. "There were several stories circulating on social media last night about a gang in Manhattan. At 0430 hours, we received a 911 call and sent four officers to investigate. They were attacked, and fought back. I've just finished reviewing the footage from their body cameras. Ladies and gentlemen, I hate to confirm that two officers are currently in hospital and two more are dead. We are presently unsure exactly what they were fighting."

The gathered officers erupted with exclamations. Richards held up his hands to quiet them, and waited briefly.

"Whoa, hold your horses," Richards said. "Our officers shot a couple of their guys, and they are in the morgue, too. The dead guys, and I can't believe I'm telling it like this...the dead perps are covered in blood, some of it is dried and caked so we know it was there a while. They all have injuries that we can't explain just yet. All we could see from the body cam footage before the cameras got obscured by blood was people growling and snarling in what sounded like a scene out of a...a zombie movie. I won't have any more details until the medical examiner is finished." The assembled officers began murmuring again. Morgan looked over at Skelter. He raised his eyebrows at her, then sipped at his coffee.

Commander Richards continued, "The other problem right now, is that we are in the middle of New Year's Eve preparations. We've got about forty-eight hours to calm things down as the city gears up for the biggest outdoor party of the season. It's all hands on deck from right now until it's all over. Because of the attacks this morning, we're implementing the City Emergency Response Plan, and we're all going to work together to make sure New Year's Eve goes off like it's supposed to."

Morgan looked toward the commander with questions on her face. He nodded back to her, indicating he'd fill her in as soon as the briefing was over. He issued assignments, and ended with a warning. "Look, we don't know what we're facing here. Be extra careful. Everyone on the street, or in a patrol vehicle, or on horseback better be in body armor. I've also authorized extra ammunition for each of you."

Skelter looked at Morgan as officers left the room to start their shift. "Zombies?" he mouthed. Morgan shrugged and headed to the end of the room where Commander Richards was gathering his paperwork.

"I know you are here investigating about cyber crime, but I'm going to need your help," Richards said without any preamble.

"Tell me what you need, and we will help. We are based out of your office, provided by your good will, and we've got some good tech available, too," Morgan said.

Richards thought for a moment, then said. "Can you get up in the air? Using drones around Manhattan is possible, of course, but with all the tall buildings, decorations, and ticker tape it's a bigger challenge than I need right now. Plus, I'd like to get every person I can out on the street and that includes my drone team. I'd appreciate if you could leverage that FBI chopper you've got, and visit an incident that's going on right now."

Morgan breathed deliberately and slowly. She wasn't a big fan of flying, and it only had a little do with being shot at in a chopper on a previous mission, then getting herself shot in an incident later that same week. Skelter stepped up and said, "We can have that chopper here and be in the air in thirty minutes, Commander."

Chapter Two

Morgan and Skelter headed to their office to grab some gear. She had not told Skelter, nor any of the Americans, about her psychic ability to listen in to conversations that weren't within hearing range. It was a skill she had leveraged well on previous missions, but it wasn't something she wanted to advertise because she felt that more people knowing about it would put her at more risk than usual. Besides, how exactly do you tell people, *hey, I have this creepy ability to hear at great distances, even through walls.* The people that knew her best knew, including her boss at the agency, and James, and only a very small number of additional people knew. She preferred to keep her secrets close.

The chopper that arrived was a sleek, brand new Bell, with an experienced pilot and two FBI members in tactical gear. Morgan and Skelter met with the pilot and two tactical officers for a quick briefing. After introductions, Morgan explained what they knew, which wasn't much, including the circumstances of the police officers that had died early that morning.

"Ma'am," said Riley, the taller of the two tactical members, "Though we're called Hostage Rescue Team, or HRT, that's not all that we do. We're trained and experienced in tactics. We don't carry gear like handcuffs because we don't take prisoners so you'll have to tell us if we need people set aside for the police to pick up." He waited for Morgan's reply.

"I'm not especially interested in prisoners either, but we need to know exactly who these hooligans are, why they are keeping police officers pinned down, and try to resolve their presence before the New Year's Eve parties get started."

"So, you will want to be arresting people," Argus, the second tactical officer asked. He didn't sound bothered either way, but he clearly wanted to ensure they were all on the same page.

"That is my first choice," Morgan said, hands on her hips. "However, if the scene looks like we need to use deadly force, then we will once we have a better idea of what's happening."

"Yes Ma'am," Argus said, finally smiling. His big grin revealed a gap in the middle of his bright white front teeth, and smile lines deeply etched on either side of his closely shaved face.

"Great," said Morgan. "Then stop calling me ma'am and call me Winfeld."

The pilot was tall and serious looking, with a couple of day's worth of dark facial stubble. Morgan watched as he removed the Velcro name tag from his flight suit – Jordan it said – and then tucked it in his pocket indicating to Riley and Argus that they needed to do the same. Morgan took the helmet that Jordan offered and placed it on top of her head for the walk to the helipad, and adjusted her flak vest to fit better as she made her way down the hallway. She felt, rather than heard the two HRT agents talking, though they were at least fifteen feet behind her.

"She's feisty, Skelter told me, and a good shot," said Riley. Riley was tall and slender, with arms almost too long for his shirt once all his gear was strapped on him. His fingers were long, deft at stripping down a weapon, reloading ammunition, or playing his guitar on a rare day of solitude at home.

"Just don't develop a crush on her," Argus laughed quietly. "She's old enough to be your mom."

"Like hell, she is not," Riley said. "I'm really bad at judging age, but my mom is forty-eight and doesn't look anything like her."

15

"She's got to be in her mid-forties," Argus said. "According to what I saw on her while we flew out here, she was awarded the Victoria Cross by the Queen of England in the late 1990s. That's almost never granted outside of a war, so whatever she did was really big. The rest of the information is all classified."

"Well hell," Riley replied. "She is old enough to be my mom, I guess. A badass mom."

Morgan turned the corner to head through the door toward the helipad, registering that she had not heard the conversation in a way most people would relate to. Her extrasensory perception was turned up full blast and she was hearing their private chatter. It made her smile, even as she felt self conscious about them trying to guess her age. She knew her days as an active operative were numbered given her age, and felt a moment of gratitude for her promotion to assistant director. As they entered the chopper and turned their communication collars on, she looked at Riley and Argus and said, "Just for the record, I'm forty-five."

Argus and Riley looked at one another, wonder written across their faces. Morgan smiled at them and said, "I've got really good hearing."

Manhattan spread out elegantly as the chopper lifted, and Morgan took a moment to look at the preparations underway around Times Square. She spotted her hotel, and wondered briefly what time she'd get back to it for some sleep. It was a quick flight to get over the area where the current incident was unfolding, just a few blocks from where the officers had been attacked earlier that morning. She saw two police vehicles, doors left open and lights flashing, and garbage from an overturned dumpster littered the area.

"Where are all the people?" Morgan asked, looking out the window. "I see two police vehicles, but no public hiding, nobody wandering."

"There's the school bus...I'll radio down and see who we can connect with," Skelter said.

He spoke into his comms unit, and before long there was a shaky voice in his ear.

"I say again, this is officer Delburne, badge 6991, and we are pinned down in a store on the corner. I can see your chopper. Over."

"What's keeping you pinned down?" Skelter asked. "I can't see anything from up here. Over."

"A bunch of...of...people are on that school bus there. I...I don't know where they came from. They f...freak out if we try to leave here, but then, they quiet down when we come back into the store. We know they have at least one assault rifle. We are out of ammo, and can't return to our vehicles to restock. Over."

Morgan leaned her head against the window, trying to get a better look at the bus. "What weapons do the officers have down there?"

"Handguns," Skelter replied. "Anything else is in their vehicle."

"Jordan can you take us lower? I can see stuff smeared on the bus windows but that's it," Morgan said. "Those officers have been pinned down for more than two hours. Let's not make them wait much longer."

"Sure thing," Jordan said. He expertly descended, and the site grew clear through Morgan's binoculars.

"Looks like there's a riot on inside the bus," she said. "The windows are covered in some kind of goop – maybe paint, but they are shifting around and I can see the bus moving from the force of it."

Riley and Argus positioned their automatic weapons across their laps, and prepared to open the side doors on the helicopter. Morgan leaned over to listen to what was happening in the bus but aside from growling and crying, she couldn't pick up any conversation. She looked over to the small corner convenience store where the policemen were waiting for a rescue. She could just barely hear the buzz of them talking, though she couldn't quite catch what they were saying. Instead, she could hear the fear in their voices and it chilled her to the bone.

Jordan hovered the chopper for a few moments, and then moved closer. The passenger door of the large school bus swung open and a figure stepped out, looking at the helicopter. His arms raised and he pumped at the air as if trying to swing a punch. His mouth was wide open as he yelled, and his head was swinging angrily from side to side. It wasn't long before an equally gruesome character, with a semi automatic weapon casually hanging off a sling crossing his bloodied body, stepped off the bus to pull the first man back in.

"What...what the hell was that?" Argus stuttered into his mouthpiece. "That person was covered in blood. Looks like something out of a zombie movie."

"Alright, let's keep in mind that zombies are usually a TV thing," Morgan said slowly. "They obviously have weapons, but didn't fire at us, although we know they shot at the cops down there.

"Alright," Skelter echoed. "Zombie looking creatures on the bus. We need to get them neutralized to rescue the cops down there."

"How many people do you think are on the bus? Our sensors are picking up heat signals, but the reception is terrible and I can't figure out how many people there are," Riley said tensely.

"We don't know," Skelter said.

Morgan looked at Riley. "Let's fire a volley of shots into the hood of the bus, not trying to shoot anyone at this point, and see if we can draw their attention."

Riley fired three rounds into the hood. Though no one came out of the bus, the team on the chopper could see the bus rocking from side to side as more movement erupted in response to the shooting. A side window opened and the muzzle of a weapon pointed at them. Morgan's heart hammered in her ears as her hearing caught up with the action. She heard the weapon being cocked, and listened as orders to draw weapons were growled inside the bus. Morgan raised her handgun and turned slightly so she could get a good shot. She fired three rounds, knocking the shooter backwards.

Riley and Argus looked at Morgan with questions on their faces, ready to do more as soon as she gave the word. Morgan nodded curtly, and motioned to Riley to get ready for a rapid descent. Riley passed his rifle to Morgan. "Hold that," he said to Morgan. "This will give you a better shot, not that you need it obviously, but if I am getting shot at on the way down, I'd rather you were using a rifle to take them out a little easier than you can with your handgun. I'm going to use a small rocket launcher from the ground to hit the bus."

Jordan maneuvered the chopper a little farther from the bus, expertly keeping it steady as Riley hung two small rocket launchers around his neck. Riley gave a thumbs up to Argus, ready to be lowered with the winch.

Once Riley was on the ground, he fired at the bus, rapidly changed weapons, and fired again. He called to Argus, who quickly hit the retract button on the winch. As Riley was hoisted back up to the chopper, the yellow of the bus was obscured by a pair of fireballs that melded into one giant plume, scorching cars, buildings, and a few spindly trees that stood in the boulevard.

As the explosion settled into a raging fire, the police officers emerged from hiding in the corner store with their thumbs up toward the chopper. They ran to the police car to replenish their ammunition. They grabbed shotguns, but there was no real need. Nothing and nobody had emerged from the blast.

On the chopper, the team looked at one another, and nodded at Riley on the efficiency of his aim, though not in a jolly sort of way. There was no telling what the death toll was, nor any way of knowing who or what had been on the bus.

"From the ground," Riley said, quietly, "There was nothing to see. Whatever they coated the insides of that bus with blocked the windows completely."

"The forensics reports will tell us plenty, and hopefully won't take long," Morgan said. Everyone was quiet for the rest of the trip, lost in their own thoughts.

Chapter Three

"Okay, Skelter, I'll grant you that it looked like a zombie apocalypse, but let's try not to get ahead of ourselves here," Morgan said. She took the large cup of coffee that Skelter handed her.

"That looked like an episode from bad TV," Skelter said.

"There has to be an explanation for it," Morgan said. They were in the break room back at the police station, preparing for New Year's Eve and their assignment, but still distracted by the morning's incident.

Skelter's phone buzzed with a new message. It was from the local medical examiner, and she wanted to update them along with the station commander.

"Look," Dr. Fleury said as they entered the morgue. "I know this is a big deal and so I want you to know we're doing everything we can to find out what was going on with the attack on the police officers early this morning, and then this bus incident. There is a lot of debris on the bus, and it was a biohazard zone in there, as you can imagine. There's not much left of the bodies, but it looks like there are at least a dozen sets of remains, and this is also interesting." She held up several evidence bags, some with small plastic packages shaped liked teardrops, and another bag with teardrops that had been opened. There was also a large bag of pills.

"I'm pretty sure the pills are Fentanyl or some derivative of it. Deadly, as you know. What I'm curious about is what's in these other vials. It's liquid. It's in an interesting package. See how it looks like a teardrop, and there is a small scoring near the top? That's so it can easily be torn open, and then liquid gets administered under the tongue for fast absorption. We've seen some like this in the past where diehard drug addicts were actually putting liquid substances onto their eyes, up their nose, you name it. I don't know what the drug in these is yet."

"Doctor, have you seen this here in New York before?" Skelter asked.

"Nope, not in packaging of that shape. There was some talk at a conference recently, of some new drug coming out of Asia in creative packaging, but this is the first I've seen of it. They called it *Joy19* at the conference. I'm going to reach out to some colleagues and see what we can piece together."

"How did these survive the bus blast?" Morgan asked, looking at the debris that was carefully laid out on several tables in the morgue.

"They came inside of that heavy duty case there. It was broken open but not really damaged in the blast. Average street drug dealers don't protect their stuff like that. It'd be too heavy to move around, for the speed they normally act with."

"So are you thinking that these guys were higher up the chain than street dealers?" Morgan chewed on her bottom lip as she contemplated what could be going on.

"Maybe," the medical examiner said. "There's another weird thing you need to know."

Morgan, Skelter, and Commander Richards looked on expectantly. Morgan's hair began to stand up along the back of her neck.

"We found remains, just hands and forearms, attached to handcuffs that were connected to the frame of the bus. The bones are on the small side, the size of teenager probably. It looks like there were two or maybe three of them and they were being held in that bus."

Back at the police station, Morgan reached out to James at the ACTI office in London, England. "James, I'm sorry to wake you. Tomorrow is New Year's Eve and we have some disturbing incidents leading up to it. It looks like some heavy duty street drugs are involved, and there may have been captives in the bus incident this morning. Young captives, but we won't know for sure for a while – it'll be days before the medical examiner can get through everything."

She paused while he replied, and then repeated part of the conversation for Skelter's sake.

"You're able to coordinate with the people here so you can help analyze these drugs? That would be a big help. The morgue and staff there are focussed first on the dead bodies as you can imagine. The coroner did mention that there was a drug in similar packaging called *Joy19* that they talked about at a conference. See what you can find out about that, too."

"Well, they've seen the stories on British news about a gang trying to take over Manhattan," she said when she hung up, "and some mention of zombies."

After catching a quick four hour sleep in her lavish hotel room, Morgan returned to the police station on New Year's Eve morning just as her phone rang. She pressed the speaker button so Skelter could listen in.

"Your sample of that drug is quite interesting," James said in Welsh accented English, tinged with fatigue. "It's a drug we haven't seen over here yet. It's got compounds we don't normally see mixed together. I spoke with Dr. Fleury and she said that some of the victims also had significant alcohol in their blood streams."

"Like drinking booze to get an accelerated reaction?" Skelter asked.

"Could be," James said, "since that's common practice now. Or maybe it's to obscure the taste. I'd recommend watching what kind of drink that people are consuming at New Year's Eve parties where you also expect drug activity. It might be that they have already had a head's up that there is something new to try, and they'll be looking for it."

Morgan rubbed her right temple with the tips of her fingers. She was tired and hungry, and she could feel her stomach distracting her. She was thinking of the captives on the bus. Were they drug dealers in training? Kids snatched off the streets and then being tortured or heavily drugged before being released on the streets to sell drugs? Were they injected with drugs to keep them docile and compliant, put into a stupor so their captors could do horrible things like brand and disfigure them without a bunch of noise? Torture, and keeping them hidden wasn't hard to pull off from a cheap motel with a 'do not disturb' sign on the door. Moving them out of the neighbourhood on New Year's Eve would have been easy among all the chaos and partying, especially since they had a bus.

Morgan gathered her coat and gloves. She nodded to Skelter to let him know she was ready to head to a briefing with local law enforcement, social workers, and a couple of city psychologists who were going to be on the ground tonight for the festivities. The command centre, and meeting place, was set up in police headquarters just around the corner from the station they were working from.

"Let's stop and grab a sandwich on the way over," Morgan said. "I'm starving."

Skelter nodded, his black knitted cap standing out sharply against the grey hair at his temples and his pale face.

"You okay?" Morgan asked as they stepped outside and a blast of icy winter air hit them.

"Starving," he replied. "I just needed you to say the same."

"You shouldn't wait for me to eat. I get focussed on what I'm doing and forget. One of the things I like about New York is that there's food everywhere to remind me."

Morgan stepped up to the counter and ordered pastrami with provolone and pickles on dark rye. Along with the mustard the deli made, it had become her favorite sandwich. They carried their wrapped lunches to the meeting and set them out on the table in front of them. Morgan ignored the looks from others who watched the muscled, fit woman tackling her meal with no concern about calories or carbs.

The briefing started with comments from the medical examiner, who didn't hold back.

"We've established that there is a mix of drugs in the suspects shot by police, and though we're getting less information from the remains on the bus, there were protected packages of drugs that didn't get damaged and we are analysing them. It looks like there were prisoners on that bus, likely abduction victims. We're looking through missing persons records but it's possible they aren't even reported missing yet. Those remains are from children between the ages of twelve and fifteen." She turned the podium over the police chief.

"The children were young, and we are comparing the information we have with missing person reports but that's going to take some time so we've also got people scouring social media. In the meantime, we've got things organized and working well for tonight's festivities. Here are a few things you need to note," he said. Morgan looked around the room to get a sense of who was listening.

As she and Skelter left the briefing, Morgan tossed her sandwich wrapper into a garbage can. "Skelter, I can't get rid of this feeling that something bad is going down tonight."

"Probably just the anticipation of a New Year's Eve here in the Big Apple, isn't it? And don't try to convince me otherwise, because I don't need anymore cynicism than I am already chewing on."

"Hmm," she grunted. *My spidey senses are in overdrive*, she thought.

They stopped at a hotel ballroom near the police station. Early party goers were drinking among an abundance of short skirts, high heels, and plastic sparkling tiaras. The smell of alcohol filled the crowded room. "These are some of the folks that come into the area early in the day so they can escape the traffic as it gets worse. They'll be completely drunk or even passed out before midnight arrives," the officer with them said. He was in his late thirties, with an impeccable uniform, freshly buzzed hair, and held his cap tucked under his left arm.

"Sergeant Platt," Morgan said, looking closely at him. "Were you in the military before joining the police force?"

"Yes, Ma'am," he said, a smile creasing the lines beside his mouth as the light hit his brown eyes. "Thirteen years. How'd you guess?"

"Something about your bearing, uniform, your whole presentation. What made you become a police officer?"

He bent his left leg, putting his knee forward so that his foot dangled, and tapped his shin with his opposite hand. "Lost the bottom of this leg in a bombing and retired from the marines. I was able to get work on the police force once I proved I could keep up with everyone else."

"Impressive," Skelter said. "You don't limp."

"I was lucky," Platt said. "I had an amazing doctor who was able to create a perfect stump, and a couple of follow up surgeries helped. Then I worked with the world's meanest, nastiest physiotherapist in Ireland. She nearly killed me, but I don't limp, and I can run on it for short distances." He smiled, and the lines around his eyes crinkled.

"Did you do your rehab at a little farm outside of Dublin? With someone named Rebecca?" Morgan asked, astonished.

"Yeah, you know her?"

Morgan nodded. "Yup, I still send her a lump of coal and a bag of brittle every month to remind her of me."

Platt chuckled. "She is one fierce woman. Looks all sweet and kind, then she takes your feelings and turns them into hate and anger."

Morgan felt her stomach do a little flip as she looked at Platt. He was easy to like. Then she waved to him and Skelter to indicate it was time to get moving. The three of them patrolled parties, stopped to watch revellers on back streets, and ducked into dark lanes. Morgan managed to do some listening, and while there were a few clips of conversation about drugs, and an occasional waft of weed to wander through, most comments were about buying more alcohol or how cute someone was.

The energy and excitement among the crowd was high as midnight came closer. People pressed together to be able to watch the famous ball drop. Loudspeakers crackled and music roared. Morgan could feel the light from the billboards on every corner, the sides of buildings, and the tops of subway station entrances. The intensity of colour added to the noise and chaotic nature of it all. She watched as a couple of hooded figures approached an older looking gentleman on a corner.

"Take a look," she said to Skelter and Platt. "Drug deal, or robbery?"

"Let's get closer," Platt said, and they prepared to cut across the busy street.

The elderly gentleman was ready, however. He looked at the two approaching him, nodded his head to say hello and waved with the bottom of his walking stick, the glint of an anti-slip device unmistakable to the hooded figures. They gave him a wide berth, and melted into the crowd.

"You okay, Sir?" Platt said as he approached the man.

"Oh yeah, of course. Ain't fit to be in New York if you can't keep a sharp eye," he said.

"You from around here?" Platt asked, "used to being in a crowd?"

"Yeah, of course. I live in Hell's Kitchen, right down the street."

"Alright then, Sir, you have a good time tonight. Happy New Year," Platt said.

Morgan looked at Platt as the man made his way through the crowd and more people surged toward the ball that would drop at midnight. "He okay?" she asked.

"Yeah, he's a resident. He's fine. It's the visitors that are going to be most vulnerable, I think," Platt said.

They continued along. People were enjoying the music and fun of the night. Midnight came and the big ball dropped, ticker tape shot out and flooded the streets. It quickly combined with random piles of snow to make a sodden, slippery mess along the gutters.

Their headsets crackled at the same time. "Team seven, report to corner A. There's some kind of incident. Over."

The emergency response plan didn't waste time with names or street addresses. Each corner, common stop, and subway sign had been assigned a letter reference so responders could get to an incident before the public got in the way with their cell phone cameras and questions. Morgan, Skelter, and Platt sprang into action and headed to the location a short distance away. There, at the end of an alley was a scene unlike anything they could have prepared themselves for.

Morgan listed off commands into her headset. The hair stood up on her arms and the back of her neck. "We need a tactical squad, immediately, and ambulance," she called.

A male lay prostrate on the ground covered in blood and moaning. His winter coat was spread open, and his hat was askew. Except it wasn't his hat, but his neck that was askew, Morgan realized. The hat was still properly on his head. Another figure, a young woman in a pink faux fur jacket, open at the front and revealing a silver sparkling dress, was limping and pacing nearby. One of the spiked heels from her pleather boots had broken off. Her eyes were wide, her face in a grimace. She was breathing quickly.

"Are there others?" Skelter yelled at her, trying to see further down the alley but unable to make out anything among the garbage bins and dim light. "Is it just the two of you?"

A clanging noise down the lane caught their attention. The woman screamed but didn't flee. She couldn't keep her eyes from the man on the ground, and suddenly bent down over him, sinking her teeth into the flesh of his broken neck. Noise from down the alley intensified like a dog in the throws of an attack.

"What the hell," Platt exclaimed. "I want to shoot her, but I'm not sure it won't just piss her off!"

"Well, we don't have any means to tranquilize her!" Skelter shouted.

"And I don't have authority to kill here, unless as a last resort, but I will." Morgan said, pulling her Glock from her shoulder holster. She was listening for sounds down the alley. Crying, whimpers, and moaning sounds made their way up the brick walls that fenced the lane. "Go for a non-lethal shot."

Platt shot a bullet just inches in front of the woman's head, where she was still ripping at the flesh of the body in front of her. The bullet made a chunk of cement fly out of the ground and it startled her enough that she looked up, snarling and baring her bloody teeth in Platt's direction. She lifted herself slightly to launch toward him. He fired again and the bullet struck her shoulder. She stopped briefly as if to wave off the impact of the round, then leaned forward, steadying herself.

Skelter had his gun pointed at her forehead. The woman snarled and looked toward the guns pointed at her. She jumped over the body but didn't lift her feet high enough, stumbled, but didn't fall. Morgan fired and the woman fell face first on the ground a short distance in front of them.

"There are more of them in the alley," Morgan said, "I can hear them."

"I can't hear a damn thing now my ears are ringing," Platt said.

"Behind the dumpster, on the left," Morgan said.

The three of them entered the alley with weapons drawn, offering coverage for each other as they went along. Skelter moved up, then Platt, and Morgan came up on the rear, watching behind them as Skelter and Platt looked ahead. They approached the dumpster just as a tactical unit arrived at the opening to the lane where the faux fur woman and the man lay. Two of the tactical unit members came up to

Morgan as she waved them in and spoke quickly. "We don't know how many are up here yet."

As they reached the dumpster, five people, not dead but looking like dishevelled and broken leftovers of a brawl, were sprawled on the ground. Not one of them appeared able to stand; there was moaning, and then the unmistakeable sound of someone throwing up.

"Judging by the first two we saw, we may not have much time before these ones go into zombie mode and start ripping us apart," Skelter said.

"We need to secure them and make sure they can't do that," Morgan said. "It would help if at least one of them lives so we can question them and figure out what's going on."

They huddled for a moment, assigning the pickup and transport of the group to the tactical team. The tactical group surrounded the muddled mass. Moaning and hissing in the group subsided noticeably as individuals were turned over, handcuffed, shackled, and in acknowledgement to the faux fur coat woman, the officers strapped masks on to prevent biting.

Morgan's headset squawked with a report from police dispatch. There was another incident a few blocks to the east of them, along the border of Central Park. It was 0200 hrs as Morgan and her team jogged toward the incident.

There were four additional scenes that Morgan, Skelter, and the inexhaustible Platt responded to into the morning. When they dragged themselves into the police station, Commander Richards looked them over, and shook his head. "Rough night," he said. "Coffee's ready in the break room. Grab one and come to the briefing room. We start in five minutes."

Morgan felt as though her feet were moving through wet cement as she made her way to the coffee pot. Then she looked at Platt and wondered how he did it. His stump had to be sore after nearly twenty-four hours in his prosthesis and the night they'd had, but he wasn't complaining.

"I have a secret," he said.

"Don't tell me it's some kind of magic drug." Morgan said. "I don't think I could take it."

"You like coffee, right?" he said, reaching into the back of a cupboard.

"Like?" Skelter laughed. "She mainlines coffee."

"It's better that I drink coffee and not scotch at this time of day," Morgan said grumpily.

"Add this to your cup, and then pour the coffee on top of it," Platt said. He handed her a jar of instant espresso as confusion and curiosity overtook Morgan's face.

"Instant espresso? Added to drip coffee?" she said.

"Yeah, just try it," Platt said.

Morgan was too tired to argue. She added a small spoonful of the espresso to her oversized cup and then poured hot coffee over it. The smell filled her nostrils and she savoured the moment to allow the scent to kickstart her brain. After adding a healthy plop of cream and four lumps of sugar to her cup, Morgan took a little taste and looked at Platt.

"That's perfectly awful," she said, grimacing.

"But it's also perfect," he laughed.

They headed back to the briefing room. Morgan nodded to Platt to take the last chair and he gratefully sat down as she and Skelter leaned on the wall at the back of the room.

"It's been a hell of a New Year's Eve," the commander started. Reports of zombies were spreading widely on social media. "In order to stop the spread of panic, none of you will use the term zombie, despite what the public may call it. We know that what is happening is some kind of reaction to a drug and it's sending people into a rage...

or…or, or delirium…where, yes, they are biting other people and we aren't sure why."

"Any word on the people that were picked up at the alley?" Morgan asked. "The five of them were pretty wasted and didn't seem to have the energy to take anyone on."

"We think maybe that's an early stage of the drug reaction," Commander Richards said. "They were quiet while being transported to the hospital, and then as the hours have passed, two of them went totally berserk. Since they were in the hospital and well restrained, they weren't able to do much harm, but we haven't had word yet of a drug that can restrain them or keep them calm until this stuff wears off."

Back in their office, Skelter and Morgan sat quietly contemplating the news from the briefing. Platt joined them, silently offering Morgan and Skelter another of his espresso laced coffees.

"Sure sounds like zombies, even though it's not," Skelter said quietly.

"There's still no such thing as zombies," Morgan said, elbow on the table and her chin sitting on her upturned hand. "I'm going to call James and see what he's heard."

While Morgan called James, Skelter and Platt spoke quietly in the corner. "If these reactions to the drug are delayed, and the dosages are small, it could be spreading all over the city and that will make it a lot harder to figure out who is behind it," Platt said.

As she disconnected the phone, Morgan turned her attention to her colleagues. "There were a couple of people picked up at La Guardia Airport with a plastic envelope of teardrop shaped packets – presumably *Joy19* – hidden between the screen and case of a laptop, and in fake laptop batteries. They got picked up on a luggage x-ray, not because you can see the drugs, because you can't. A curious luggage screener started looking when he noticed a battery that had a crooked screw trying to hold it together, otherwise we would not have known. We have no idea how many people may have made it through airport screenings with this stuff."

"Well if it's coming here from somewhere else, they could be distributing it as they travel," Platt offered.

"Or, maybe it's a recipe they can create here, like meth," Skelter said.

Commander Richards entered their office. "More news, not necessarily good. One of the officers injured in the first attack said he heard from an informant, shortly before it all went down, that there is a new drug being launched on New Year's Eve. Dealers were encouraged to sell it as an edible product in things like gummy candies or mixed with vodka to mask the taste of the drug. It's supposed to create a sense of euphoria and happiness that lasts a few hours. However, it seems that several hours after taking it, some users pass out, and in others there's this crazy behaviour we're witnessing."

After the commander left, Morgan looked at Skelter and Platt. "I need to get some rest. How about if we meet back here in a few hours?"

"I just drank more coffee, and I'm too wired to rest. I'll stay here," Platt said.

"Make it a half day and I can get home to see my family for a bit," Skelter said.

"Done," Morgan replied. "Let's make it six hours and we can meet back here. Platt how about you come with me and show me where I can find some more pastrami?"

Within a half hour, Morgan and Platt were sitting in a small deli close to Central Park, their pastrami sandwiches in front of them.

"So how do you know the physiotherapist in Ireland?" Platt asked as they sat down.

Morgan hesitated just for a moment. She didn't like talking about herself, especially when doing so was inevitably going to lead to a discussion about Jake. She missed Jake every day.

"You don't have to answer if it's awkward," Platt held up a hand apologetically.

"But you want to know," she looked at him as she pulled the pickle off the top of her sandwich. "There was a lot going on at that point. I was there to recover from a gunshot wound that had left my arm immobilized."

"Did you get shot in Ireland?"

"Nope, I got shot in Canada but was working with someone who was well connected with Ireland and he recommended the clinic."

"People get shot in Canada?" he asked with mock surprise. "I'm just kidding. I know people get shot there, but I usually think of Canada as the land of peace and quiet. When I went camping in New Brunswick it was like another world compared to the crowds of New York."

"It is for the most part, but people in our line of work are always targets. How'd you wind up in Ireland? There's got to be great treatment available here."

"Ack," said Platt. "I was in Afghanistan when I lost my leg. I had bad dreams and a terrible attitude afterwards. Drank too much. My wife took the brunt of it, and I thought if I went away for some rehab it might help. Amanda filed for divorce while I was there."

"Sorry about that, I really am," Morgan said as she contemplated how to pick up her sandwich.

"She didn't deserve it," Platt said matter of factly as he regarded his oversized lunch. "She's married again and has a couple of kids. That's what she wanted."

"Hmm, that's a really damned good attitude you have there."

"You have any kids?" He took a bite of sandwich, and looked over the top of it as he waited for her answer.

"Nope, never made time for them. There was a puppy I looked after for a bit."

He laughed, choking as he inhaled crumbs from the rye bread. "It didn't work out I gather," he squeaked.

"It was temporary," she said. She looked at him and smiled, enjoying the banter. *Conversation is easy with this guy.* "I found the dog during a storm, no one claimed him right away, so I held onto him long enough to get him settled with a widower."

"Where do you live? I mean, I know you're Canadian, but it's a big place."

"I was living in Nova Scotia, but sold my condo there a few months ago. I'm based out of London, England right now."

They chatted while they ate. It felt easy, just two colleagues out for some food. Morgan sighed, and then let memories of Jake flood her brain while she headed toward the hotel and some sleep.

What would you say about zombies, Jake?

But Jake couldn't say a word about zombies. He was killed by a heart attack, while they were on a boat doing covert operations off the British coast. She could still see Jake's body in front of her, feel his warmth as she performed the systematic actions of CPR. Her work partner and potential life partner, he was gone in just a few minutes. He became a statistic adding to the proof that most heart attacks that occur outside of a hospital result in death.

Morgan decided she wasn't ready to sleep quite yet. She changed into workout clothes and locked her gun in the safe in her room before heading to the hotel gym. When she entered the low ceilinged room, there were two other guests there, but they were all following the public gym protocol with their earphones in and steadfastly ignoring one another. The room was warm, and Morgan hung her light workout jacket on the front of the treadmill, started her playlist, and stepped onto the machine, placing one foot on either side of the moveable mat before programming the workout and pushing the start button. She started at a slow pace that quickly sped up and had her jogging an incline she could soon feel in her glutes. Her music was fast paced and current, and Morgan relished the sensation of tension slipping from her mind to fuel her muscles. She tapped the button on the handrail to increase her speed and focussed on her breathing, foot placement, and the incline changes. Forty minutes later, Morgan stepped off the treadmill and grabbed her jacket. She balled it up and used it to wipe the sweat from her face and neck, paused, then pulled out the front of her t-shirt to dab the sweat from between her breasts.

Gad, I seem extra sweaty today. And my feet are screaming at me. Morgan stretched in front of the wall of mirrors that ran the length of the room and looked at herself closely, noticing the blotches on her face and neck that sometimes showed up following a good run. *Why can't I be one of those women who glows when they work out? Oh, right. Because nobody glows when they work out...I swear I am feeling every one of my birthdays today. Seems like the New Year's Eve adventures delivered a bit of an ass kicking.*

It took a while for Morgan to fall asleep in her hotel room. She had to consciously push the jagged, painful memories of Jake back into the corner of her brain where unfinished business rested. She could feel the onset of heartburn, probably the combination of running so soon after a pastrami sandwich, and decided to sit up in the easy chair instead of laying on the bed. She covered herself with a hotel blanket, set the timer on her watch, and swept away thoughts of zombies before drifting into sleep.

After her nap and a shower, Morgan returned to the police station seeking out Skelter and Platt. They were both in the office, and they looked guilty as she opened the door.

"You guys were talking about me," she said.

"No, no we weren't," Skelton stammered.

"You were, and you shouldn't," she said tensely.

"My fault," Platt said. "I was just saying it was nice to have a sandwich earlier and not be thinking about drug addled, nearly dead people that are not zombies."

Morgan sat down with a coffee that she had picked up in in the hotel café, and carefully removed the lid while the aroma filled her nostrils. *I really wish you were scotch, and not just a big cup of coffee. I could really use some booze.*

By the time the evening briefing was completed, and they added the updates from London, Morgan's team had lots of information to work with. Incidents of bizarre behaviour were being reported from along the eastern seaboard, south as far as Florida, and west toward the middle states. Small cities declared states of emergency as their first responders and emergency rooms were overwhelmed. By the third of January with no end in sight, the President declared a state of emergency in America. Reports of strange and similar incidents in Canada, Germany, and Britain were reported, and more declarations followed.

"I have little experience with a drug issue like this, so we need your input here," Morgan said, nodding at a small team of DEA agents that joined them.

One of the agents, Angelo Reddy, shrugged his shoulders. "I don't know what to tell you. This thing may sputter out as word gets out and users shy away from trying the drug, but that's not the way it usually works. We know that a couple of the guys high up in the drug organizations in New York have been killed by zombies, but we don't know who else is involved yet."

"We're trying not to call anyone a zombie," Morgan said, trying to sound patient instead of patronizing. "If you want the public to go nuts, you can use the term, but I don't think it's going to help one bit."

Darryl Shaltz, the other DEA agent, snorted. "If you check social media, or go into any coffee shop here in the neighborhood, everyone's talking about zombies. You know, if it walks like a duck, talks like a duck, then it's a duck."

When Morgan looked at Skelter with her eyebrows raised, he jumped into the conversation. "The police have asked us not to use the word zombie. We need to get to the bottom of this and keep it in perspective in order to help these people who are victims of a horrible drug reaction."

"Well, what are you going to call the people who don't seem to have taken the drug but are getting attacked by the ones who did? What if they start acting like zombies too? Cops in Berlin and London are calling the perps zombies. Same in Canada," Shaltz said. "Face it, this is a zombie outbreak. Period."

"There aren't any 'second generation' victims that we know of. That's not a thing. There are sick people attacking others, but the attacked don't turn into anything. Most of them end up dying from blood loss," Platt clarified.

"We're moving you folks to the control centre," said a young police officer entering the room unannounced. "The boss wants you to work closer with the military as this unfolds."

"Done," said Morgan. "Let's go. We're not getting anywhere on our own here."

When she entered the control centre, Morgan was greeted by the Director of the FBI, Roger Bilous, and Colonel Andrew Black of the U.S. Marines. *They look ready for action, more so than the DEA agents. Maybe we can make a dint in this after all,* she thought.

"We need to bring some firepower in on this," Colonel Black was saying. "We're not going to extinguish this situation by just watching what's going on."

"Agreed, so let's talk about the best places to direct our efforts," Director Bilous said.

Morgan looked at the men in front of her. Black was a big man, his skin the colour of dark chocolate, and she could see his upper arm muscles putting pressure on his uniform jacket. She wondered briefly what kind of a workout routine he had because for a man who had to be in his mid-50s, he looked like he could win any competition he wanted.

Director Bilous was about the same age, over six feet tall, and had a light build. He moved constantly, with little hand gestures and tapping fingers. His rugged face was lined, and he had clearly been sporting a beard recently given the white of his lower face compared to the tan on his forehead. He grunted as he sat at the conference table.

The light bounced off Colonel Black's bald head as he spoke. "The state of emergency gives us lots of latitude to act, and I'd rather not send my people in on exploration if they need to be ready for a firefight."

"We've found that guns are the only way to stop affected people on the street. We've had plenty of shooting incidents," Morgan said. "However, these folks are very hard to stop. The rage, or delirium, or whatever you want to call it, that we've seen so far is...well, it's staggering. A bullet to the head or heart is necessary to stop them, and if you just wound them it's like poking a bear."

"What kind of pockets of people are we finding these folks in? Big groups? Small ones? Are they deliberately hiding, or out in the open?" Bilous' eyebrows raised as he reviewed the images Morgan shared on the projection screen.

"Small groups so far. We've seen a couple of groups of up to 15, one we blew up on a bus and another we had to blow up in a building, but most incidents are one to five people." Morgan said.

"How many police or emergency responders have been hurt?" Black asked.

Skelter answered in the same direct, unemotional voice that Black and Bilous had perfected. "We had police officers hurt almost as soon as this started, two dead and two injured the first day, and some bitten since the initial incidents. So far, we've had reports of at least eight emergency response and hospital personnel who've been attacked at small regional hospitals."

Colonel Black said, "We need to know where these things are holed up so we can go in and neutralize them."

"Things?" Police Commissioner Richards echoed.

"Things like zombies that we aren't calling zombies," Black said, his face serious.

"Right," Richards replied, "And keeping in mind these are American citizens, they are parents and children."

"Yeah, I get that, but we also need to end this before these things take over and we are living in an apocalypse movie," Bilous returned.

"It's not really like a zombie movie anyway," Shaltz said. "They aren't creating a second generation zombie by biting someone who didn't take the drugs, at least not that we're aware of. It's not like that British comedy they made. What was that called?"

"Shaun of the Dead," Platt said drily.

"Yeah, that's it," Shaltz said, "they made it into a comedy but it wasn't a topic to joke about. There's nothing funny about this at all."

"Before you blow everything out of proportion...hmm, maybe it's not possible to blow this out of proportion, because it's already so weird...anyway, our plan has to be to shut down the spread of these drugs, and the reactions to them, and to protect the integrity of the United States," Colonel Black said.

"We also have worldwide contamination to deal with. So far we're hearing of episodes in countries we are allies with, but when this hits places without much of a police or military capability to respond, it's going to get bad fast," Morgan said.

"Then we're going to implement every international protocol we can, while sending teams out to help wherever we can after we get the U.S. under control. It's time to call the President and world leaders so they are up to date," Bilous said.

Morgan called Chief Commander Steeves at ACTI. "This has become a full on military and FBI managed incident here. I'd like to get back to London as soon as possible, but in the meantime, you'll need to be in on the briefings to the world leaders. We'll have to wait to return to the cyber crime portfolio after this gets managed."

Morgan looked at Platt and Skelter. "It looks like I'll be heading back to England the day after tomorrow. We should plan some kind of farewell bash before I have to pack and then get on my way."

"You two need to come to my place, meet my family. How about tomorrow night? That'll give me time to prep tonight," Skelter said.

"Prep?" Morgan said. "Don't fuss, we just need to have somewhere to say we had some family time during all this madness, and to say so long."

"By prep I mean make sure my wife knows and that only one of us calls to have something delivered. I've messed this up before and we've both called the same place to order dinner and had two meals. The kids ate leftover pizza for an entire week, so they were okay with it, but Jenna was pissed."

"You're on," said Platt. "I never say no to somebody else cooking."

They spent the rest of the afternoon following up on implementation of emergency response plans and dispatching teams to trouble areas, including a couple of known drugs dens in rural New York state.

"There's something else about this I really don't like," Morgan said to Platt when they were alone in the office. Skelter had left for his evening at home. Colonel Black and Director Bilous had left for Washington, DC where they would have the president's ear and quick access to resources as they were needed. Commander Richards was in his office getting ready to brief the police commissioner and mayor.

"What's that?" Platt said, his prosthetic leg resting on an upturned waste bin.

"Well, what if these soldiers and cops are running around and just start shooting without really knowing who they are looking at? I think we are going to hear about people getting killed on speculation, where someone thinks they are exhibiting signs of a drug reaction, but they really aren't."

"You're talking about hyperactive response? That could get bad...that kind of stuff leads to mass murder, even genocide."

"Yeah. What if these tactical teams are going into neighbourhoods of known drug problems and they are using this crisis as an excuse to take down known drug thugs that are not, you know...part of whatever this is."

Platt let out a long slow breath and swept his hand through his hair. "How can we stop it at this point? There've been calls of drug reactions in forty communities in New York alone, and there's only just so much arresting and inquiring we can do."

"It's been bugging me since the HRT guys came to help with the bus. When they made it very clear they don't carry handcuffs because they don't take prisoners. They take people out."

Platt looked at Morgan. She could feel his eyes searching her without even looking at him. His words made her snap her head up and look at him angrily.

"There's probably nothing we can do about it if we are going to get ahead of it and stop the spread," he said.

"Nothing at all?"

"Can you think of anything?"

"Short of arresting them all and incarcerating them to wait for the drugs to wear off? There's just too many of them." She sighed and her shoulders drooped.

"Then we're stuck with the best case scenario we can hope for. Let's go grab something to eat."

"I'm not hungry," Morgan said, suddenly exhausted. "I think I'll just head back to the hotel and sleep."

"I'll walk you over. You look too tired to be reliably able to get there."

"I'm fine, Platt. I can look after myself."

"I know you can, I've seen you. Maybe I want you to protect me."

They left the building together, and the wind battered them as they rounded the first corner. "Frick, it's cold," Morgan said.

"It's January. What were you expecting?" Platt laughed.

"Not this. When I was up in Fort McMurray, I expected it."

"Where is Fort McMurray?"

Morgan explained that Fort Mac, as it was commonly referred to, was a city in northern Alberta. She had to do a bit of describing for Platt to picture where it was in his mind.

"Head east of Alaska, and then a tiny bit south," she said before pulling it up on her phone to show him.

"I know I should probably have a better idea of how Canada is laid out," he chuckled. "I think it's because our school textbooks just show the American parts of the globe. There's the U.S., then a bunch of white space, then Alaska."

When they reached her room, Morgan invited Platt in and picked up a bottle of scotch and two glasses from the sideboard.

"Whew," Platt said giving a low whistle. "This place is nice. I had no idea you were so well set up here or I would have visited sooner."

"I haven't spent much time in it. The view is great, the hotel is gorgeous, and they provide clean glasses for the booze."

Platt pulled the loveseat in front of the window so they could enjoy the view.

Morgan sat beside him and poured two glasses, offering him one.

"Are you plying me with alcohol?" he asked, suddenly looking sheepish.

"I might be," she said, no longer feeling tired. "Would you like to be plied?"

"Yes," he replied without hesitation.

They sat back against the cushions and took in the view of Manhattan, including the Empire State Building. "It is a fascinating city," Morgan said. "Full, and crazy busy. Have you lived here long?"

"Not in the grand scheme of things, no. I started out in Montana, but I was all over the place with the military. Thought I would join the police force here and be close to my parents who were living upstate at the time. They've both since died."

"No siblings?"

"Not anymore. I had an older brother who joined the Marines. Killed in action in 2000." Platt lifted his glass in salute to his brother, and drank the rest of his scotch.

"Sorry to hear that. You've had a lot of loss," Morgan said, topping up his glass.

"Probably same as you, I'm betting," Platt replied.

"Maybe. I like to ignore all that and keep it carefully closed behind a brick wall. Instead, I want you to tell me your first name, since if we are going to sleep together tonight, I should stop calling you Platt."

"We're sleeping together?"

"Well it's unlikely you'll be able to walk steadily given another scotch or two, and I am leaving soon. Are you up for a farewell fling with no strings attached?"

"As long as it's not going to make things awkward tomorrow," he said.

"Not at all," she said. "And if it does make things awkward it doesn't matter, on account of me leaving." Morgan turned toward him, and kissed him. Her lips parted slightly and her tongue met his, the mingling of scotch and heat sending a surge through her. She pulled away from him, stood up from the couch, and removed her gun from its holster so she could lock it away.

"My name's Rob," he said in a gravelly voice. Rob followed her across the room and added his weapon to the safe, followed by two

44

knives, and a small pistol that was strapped to this prosthesis. Morgan smiled at him, impressed with the armory he carried.

She locked the safe, and turned toward him. She closed her eyes as she leaned in to kiss him again, feeling his roughened hand moving down her arm.

"Do I see robes in that closet?" he said, peering over her shoulder.

"Yup, a perk of the hotel and handy for the hot tub in the next room. Want to try one on?"

Chapter Four

The next morning, Morgan got a text from Skelter while she sat in the hotel café with Rob Platt, and a cup of coffee.

Where are you?

On my way. 5 mins.

Briefing with Richards
started 5 mins ago.

Sorry. Distracted. Still going to
take me 5 mins.

Pick me up a coffee & cookie.
Better bring some for Richards, too
if you want to make up for
being late. Chocolate's good.

When Morgan and Platt walked into the briefing room, the throng of officers leaving nearly knocked the coffee from Morgan's hands. She moved to put her back against the wall while Platt held the door open.

"Sorry to be late," Morgan said as she handed Skelter and Commander Richards their coffee and cookies.

"You know," Richards said, trying to hide a smile, "You could have both come in here separately and there wouldn't be so much gossip as there will be now everyone just walked past the two of you."

"We could have," Platt said, smiling at the commander. "But sometimes it's more fun to have people know what you've been up to than to have them spreading rumours. Besides, work is intense right now and it'll give them all something else to think about."

Richards chuckled, and tried to recover by wiping at his chin before the drops of coffee made it to his neatly pressed shirt.

"The update on the outbreak is in, and it's pretty dim," Skelter said, gesturing a thanks for the coffee. "So far we've received reports of 1300 shootings by police and military from here to Europe. The numbers are expected to increase, and there are some regions that haven't reported anything though we suspect there could be issues."

"Any news from the medical community about finding some kind of cure or an antidote?" Morgan asked.

"Not yet, though they are working on it now from labs at CDC and coordinating with scientists in Canada, Switzerland, and Germany."

"Do we know how many of these shootings are really necessary? Anyone else worried about shooting first and asking questions later?" Platt asked, eyeing the group with uncharacteristic seriousness.

"We don't know," Richards said, shaking his head sadly and looking at the team. "I'm not sure we ever will, given the nature of this thing. I'm as afraid as all of you that this could easily be a way for vendettas or mass murder to be carried out."

"There needs to be some kind of criteria or something set up before police forces and military units start handing out more guns," Morgan said, the memories of Rob's caresses fading faster than she would have liked.

Morgan's mind went to the millions of people in refugee camps around the world. Then closer to people from South America and

Mexico who were being held in the United States. Even a hint of a drug reaction in those places could mean dire consequences.

Later that day, after hours on the phone tracing down leads, and a talk with Director Mullins and their boss, Commander Steeves, Morgan sat with her feet up and her head against the block wall in the control room. Platt sat at the table across from her, his leg propped up on a chair. Skelter was rubbing his eyes.

"I'm done," Skelter said. "Let's get out of here, and go eat."

As they headed to a nearby parking garage and Skelter's vehicle, he asked, "Morgan, what's up with you? You're quieter than usual."

"I'm worried," she replied. "And my inner cynic is having a heyday in my head." She didn't tell Skelter and Platt that she'd had several visions of people burning. Visions weren't an unusual thing for her, although it had been a long while since she had experienced any. Sometimes, Morgan had a hard time sorting out what was her genetically inherited psychic intuition from her overactive imagination.

"Mine too," said Platt as they climbed in Skelter's car. "Things like, could this drug have been created by a foreign government as a way to effectively kill millions of people without them having to point a gun anywhere?"

"That's where my head is leaning, too," Morgan said. "This could be a perfect plot, except that drug users in the originating country could also end up on this stuff."

"Are you serious?" Skelter said. "So you're thinking that it could be a government that doesn't care about its own citizens...of course, there are several...but who? Let's talk it out as we drive so you're not still brainstorming while my wife and kids are around."

Platt started. "Say a country – one we won't name since we aren't in a secure place – wants to make some fast headway internationally because they are sick of being ignored, or of being bullied by the superpowers, or whatever. How hard would it be for them to create a drug, get it on the market, and across any border they want?"

"If they give away the recipe to their own network of covert operators, drug lords, and put it on the web, and maybe provided some samples, it could be anywhere they want in no time at all." Skelter said quietly.

Morgan added to their thinking aloud, "And with the rate this epidemic, for lack of a better word, is spreading, is it possible they didn't realize it would have such fast consequences? Or does that even matter? The first incidents were in NYC on New Year's Eve, and people travelling home afterward were trying to smuggle drugs out in some cases, and there were delayed reactions where symptoms didn't show up until after they got home, but it's obvious the drugs were in other locations simultaneous to the New York events," Morgan said.

"Okay," said Skelter. "So, we're looking for a country with a big chip on their shoulder about the U.S., who doesn't care if the drugs spread anywhere else, including a boomerang back into their own country."

"Or didn't expect the drugs to spread like this, despite the way illegal drugs move around the globe," Morgan said. She looked out the window as they entered a residential area. It was dark and there were no children playing outside, but in her mind she could see children's outstretched arms as they reached through fences that were being overtaken by flames. She blinked to help the vision clear away.

"What if it is a country that doesn't care about their own people enough to care if a certain number of citizens die? Collateral damage as it were. How the hell will we figure out who it is?" Skelter asked.

"Well, we're fairly certain the drugs originate abroad since the medical examiner heard about those particular packages at an international conference," Platt said. "Then again, the information might have been planted at the conference to throw investigators off track."

"We know that there are several countries at the front of our minds where leaders have issued orders for mass arrests of individuals and executed them, or where governments exercise extreme control," Skelter said.

He pulled into a gated community, and zipped an access card through a reader. Halfway up the block, he turned into a driveway. His house was one of those suburban monsters, with a garage in the front obscuring most of the house behind, except for the living room window.

"Nice place Skelter," Platt said appreciatively. "I didn't know your boss paid you quite this well."

"He pays alright, but we lease this place from some famous writer for way less than market value," Skelter said. "My wife likes the gated neighborhood for the kids' sake."

"I really need to rethink what I'm doing with my life," Platt said as they walked up the sidewalk.

Skelter's children opened the door with squeals of "Daddy, Daddy!" and two kids were soon climbing up his legs. He embraced them both, and Morgan watched as he soaked up their love and hugged them tight. As she closed the front door, Morgan could see the finger and forehead prints on the glass made by the children as they waited.

Jenna was ready to greet them in the foyer, and Morgan could see a young woman floating in the background. *One of the fleet of nannies*, Morgan suspected.

Skelter leaned over to peck his wife on the cheek while she gathered coats from their guests.

"Pizza's in the den," she said. "The kids have already eaten and Lana is just waiting to take them up for baths and bedtime."

"Sorry we're late. I was hoping to be here for supper," Skelter said. He leaned in and kissed his wife on the lips and laughed as the kids made noises and guffawed at them.

Jenna laughed. "This is all good. You'll see them before bed and you've been home almost every night for the last two months, so I'll take it."

They entered the den and Morgan looked at the bookcase lined wall and vaulted ceiling. The room reminded her of the parish in Wales, where Jake had sat with his long legs draped over an aged leather armchair, talking with the old pastor while she researched her family history.

"Red or white?" Jenna asked, holding up a long stem glass.

"Neither, I'm good." Morgan smiled at her.

"She'll want scotch," Skelter said, the smile in his voice making lines around his mouth and eyes, "but I'll have some wine."

"Wine for you Rob?" Jenna asked.

"No, I'm fine thanks. I need to take some pills for my leg and I want them to go down first."

"There's chocolate milk," Judith said. "Makes the pills slide down easier, just ask the kids."

"Water's good," Platt said, smiling.

"Your leg bugging you?" Skelter asked.

"No more than usual," Platt said. "But I'm having some tests tomorrow on it and have to take a bunch of drugs to make me glow, so booze is out for tonight. They're thinking of giving me a robotic leg, and I want to impress them so I get it."

"Jenna has a special interest in robotics. She was a resident when we got married, studying with some great docs at Stanford."

"You left Stanford to marry Skelter?" Morgan asked, looking at Jenna. She took the glass offered by Skelter, and sipped it before placing it on the coffee table.

Jenna laughed, "I did, though maybe not for the reasons you are thinking. I knew medicine wasn't going to be my career but I wanted to learn about it so I had the background for writing."

"You're a writer?" Platt looked confused. "I thought you were a paramedic."

"I am doing some paramedic training because I write medical thrillers. I needed to get better acquainted with how they actually do their work."

"Do you write from home? With the kids around and everything?" Platt asked.

"They don't know I'm at home. I have a writing studio over the garage, and I close myself up in there all day."

"I wrote a book, but it's not published," Morgan said, chewing on her bottom lip. "My agent told me I should add some more polish to it – a happy ending – and so I did a little work on the text but didn't change the ending."

"That's because there is no happy ending, is that what you're trying to say?" Platt looked toward Morgan with his head tilted as if to help with his question. He was at the other end of a loveseat from her, and rubbed the top of her hand where it was sitting on the cushion.

"The lack of a fairy tale ending does have a lot to do with it," Morgan said. "My last partner died, and I wrote the book afterward in what I call my third dark period. I couldn't see how to make it into a happy ending. It's just not in me." She looked over at Platt. "You know there's no such thing as a happy ending, right?"

"Yeah, but you're the one who said zombies aren't real, and yet look what the last few days have brought," Skelter said, topping up his glass. He mouthed the words in dramatic fashion, "Zombies. Real fucking zombies."

Jenna looked at Morgan. "I bet your personal story is fascinating. Your third dark period? Zombies? Working with these practical jokers, you really should publish that book from the sound of things. Slap on a happy ending and then write a sequel from an alternate timeline that continues the story just how you want it."

When it was time to go, Morgan and Platt put on their coats and gloves near the door. Skelter said, "I could drive you back downtown, or to the train you know."

"We can take a cab Skelter, it's not a problem. It's been great to meet your wife and see you in your natural environment," Morgan said. "I'll be in touch once I'm back in London. We still have lots of work to do."

She and Platt headed for the community gate where the cab would pick them up. She grabbed Platt's arm when he slipped on a thin layer of soft snow that had been falling throughout the evening.

"I'm okay," he said.

"I didn't realize that could be your kryptonite. Snow."

"And ice," he said, "though I haven't actually fallen down in a long time. When I first got the leg it happened a lot, but I'm usually pretty good at staying upright."

"If you get approved for the new leg are you going to do more rehab in Ireland?"

"I have to commit to a whole bunch here in New York first, but I do miss that Rebecca lady, so who knows?"

"You know if you get tired of being a police sergeant, you could think about coming to work for ACTI. You might find it a little easier to do if you took on more of a background role. You'd be really useful to them with your military and police experience."

"You know as a sergeant I'm not doing that much street work...wait...are you asking me to join you over there?" Platt sounded surprised.

"Join me? Well, not specifically. I mean we had a no strings attached arrangement and I am good with that. Besides, those three dark periods relate to deaths of significant people in my life."

"Three?"

"Yup. Three periods. Four people."

"Damn," he said softly.

She shrugged and gave him a tight lipped smile. "Can't change it. But they're part of the reason I don't write happy endings."

"I like a good happy ending from time to time," Platt said ruefully. "Maybe it's time we both had one."

Chapter Five

The next morning, Morgan stood at LaGuardia Airport ready to fly back to England. She had completed her check-in, and scanned the security area as she put her ankle boots back on.

The place was brimming with people of all shapes and sizes, in all kinds of clothing. Some were obviously flying to warm places, and had donned shorts and sandals despite the cold New York temperatures. Others were in fleece pajama pants headed for international flights and hoping to sleep.

Morgan was wearing her usual bootcut jeans with stretch in the fabric, black t-shirt, and short black leather jacket. She had a scarf with images from Central Park printed on it, a gift from Jenna, loosely looped around her neck in case it was chilly on the plane. Her overcoat was the only thing she couldn't fit into the suitcase, but it was a forgiving fabric that folded up small and would fit into the overhead bin as long as people weren't trying to fit an entire closet up there. Inside her suitcase was a week's worth of clothing which all looked remarkably the same. Her signature t-shirts were mostly black, through she had one navy and one white one. She liked that they were a thick fabric instead of the transparent material she saw around her, and if anyone bothered to ask, she would have said she enjoyed how the fabric showed off her flat stomach.

When I get settled back into London I should sign up for a martial arts class and make sure I'm keeping my reflexes and technique sharp. Plus, I need to work off those pastrami sandwiches, but gawd, I'm going to miss them.

Morgan heard her name being crackled over the loudspeaker and walked over to the check-in counter.

"You have an emergency phone call from someone who says your cell phone is turned off. You'll need to check your messages," the attendant said with excruciating politeness.

I turned my phone off at security so no one would bug me, Morgan thought. *I'd rather not think about work on the flight.*

The message was from Platt, and Morgan felt a little flip in her stomach as she heard his warm voice in her ear. "Hey, I know we're not a thing like a couple or whatever, but I wanted to let you in on the news. The test this morning went well and they accepted me for the program. I'm going to be bionic this time next year! I wanted to let you know, but I also need to talk to you. Gimme a call."

That's good news, but doesn't sound like an emergency, Morgan thought as she dialled Platt's number.

"Talk fast Platt, the plane's about to board."

"Yeah, well, you heard my news in the message, right?" he sounded like an eager young kid that had just won a prize.

"Yeah and I'm happy for you. Can't wait to see you moving along on that thing and catching bad guys."

"Me too. Anyway, I want to let you know the other reason for my call...remember when we saw Grampa during New Year's Eve and we were worried about him being out in the crowds? The guy that said he lived in Hell's Kitchen?"

"Yeah I do...why?" Morgan visualized the old man they spoke with briefly on New Year's Eve. The team had worried he was about to get mugged, and watched as he held up his cane to warn two men away when they approached him.

"Can you believe that Grampa wasn't the only old guy around there? He was out with a bunch of buddies all from the home, and they were out having a very good time that night. They spread cheer all over the city."

"Gramps did? Specifically? He's usually such a loner," Morgan said, fishing for more details carefully in case anyone was listening.

"Yeah, apparently he was out for the evening with three buddies, but they got split up in the crowd so he seemed alone when we saw him, but he wasn't really. They hooked back up a short while after we saw him."

As Morgan turned her phone off again, she looked around the waiting area. People were starting to line up for the plane. She stayed near the wall, watching the crowd. She was boarding last because her ticket's late purchase and a desire to travel this early in January meant flights were crowded. Morgan's seat was one of the flip down ones at the very back of the plane.

Was the guy we saw that night a mule for transporting drugs? Or was he higher up in the scheme of things, and running a drug operation? The thought of it made her look again at the crowd. *Nearly half these passengers look over 50, and several of them are probably over 70. Senior citizens as drug dealers? But drug addicts could be dangerous for them to be around, and so could the dealers. I'm not convinced that older folks could be drug dealers and keep themselves safe, but then again....*

A man that had just joined the line of travellers was tall, older, and stood straight. He looked strong enough to do the things he wanted and needed to do. *And I suppose, if he put on a slightly tattered overcoat, changed his shoes, and carried a walking stick, he would look weak and harmless, but those two younger guys over there look more like drug traffickers.*

Morgan didn't have a lot of time to think about the potential drug traffickers once she got on the plane. She belted herself into her seat, and glanced around her. Instead of suffering from anxiety on planes like she had in the past, she had convinced herself that planes had become a guilty pleasure. There were limited conversations taking place, and people spoke in hushed tones to keep themselves isolated.

They were easy prey for her to do some eavesdropping, so she closed her eyes and listened.

"Mama, Mama, Mama," a young voice was saying.

"Yes sweetie," replied a patient mother. "What would you like?"

"I gotta pee."

Okay, I'll try another one, Morgan thought.

"Crystal, can you pass me the snacks?" A young male voice, early twenties.

"We aren't even up in the air yet," a nasal voice whined back at him. "Can't you wait?"

Next.

"Yeah, I know we have a meeting on Friday, and I'll be back by then." This was a phone call, Morgan decided.

Next.

Whispered voices, "I'll give you some to try when we get there. I can't get at any of it right now." A mature, male voice.

"I need it right now. This stuff is starting to wear off and my skin is getting itchy. Plus, I am so friggin' hungry I could eat your arm," said an agitated male voice, this one a little younger.

"Leave my arm out of it. We'll get some food for you once we're airborne. Here's some candy to tide y'over."

"I don't want candy. I want the other stuff, Mike."

"Like I said, you can have it when we get home."

Sounds like a drug conversation, Morgan thought. She sat up straight in her seat and listened closely.

"Mike, is it with your laptop? I can get it out of the overhead bin before we take off."

"Shh Ivan, stop asking. It's not with the laptop. You know how hard it was to hide that stuff so I could get it through the airport? Knock it off you fricken jerk."

"God, I really need it Mike. My mind...I think I'm losing my mind, man."

The plane moved along the runway, getting into position for takeoff.

There was growling, and a commotion, and a muffled scream from ahead as Morgan quickly unbuckled and sprang from her seat.

"Ma'am," the stewardess yelled, "Ma'am, please take your seat!"

"Fuck that," Morgan said. "Find your sky marshal if there's one on this plane."

Morgan tried to run up toward the front of the plane but the force of it accelerating made movement hard. She kept pushing, and eventually reached the front row where the scream had come from. There were only two people in the row, one of the economy styled flights where the first several rows had a tray table locked between them to make it seem roomier. Ivan, presumably, had been in the aisle seat in the front row, and had got up out of his seat, moved in front of Mike sitting in the window seat. Ivan had one knee up on Mike's lap and was trying to muffle Mike's voice with his hands while trying to grab at the flailing arm with his mouth. Morgan stood momentarily watching them, not sure how to get to Ivan in the small space. She turned herself sideways and kicked out with her right foot, catching Ivan just above the knee, forcing him to partially collapse as the joint was jolted out of place. Ivan looked toward Morgan with his eyes squinted, but still holding on to Mike's arm. A whizzing sound beside Morgan's head made her hair stand on end as the air marshal fired his taser into Ivan, while one of the leads landed in the middle of Mike's left arm.

Mike screamed, and Ivan was only partially stunned but having a difficult time coordinating his movements while trying to keep his hold on Mike's arm. Blood dripped from Ivan's mouth.

"Get back," the marshal yelled toward anyone nearby.

"Marshal, this fellow may be having a drug reaction, and he could go berserk at any second," Morgan said, then she called to the nearest stewardess, "Call this in. We'll need police and an ambulance once the plane stops."

The charge from the tazer had subsided and Mike started flailing at Ivan with his good arm.

"Get off me! Get off," Mike screamed.

Passengers were rising in their seats trying to get a good look at the commotion when Ivan, seeing an opportunity, lunged upward over top of Mike and tried to launch himself into the next row. People's arms raised up from the second row to try and hold him back, while the air marshal tried to get closer with his handcuffs.

"Marshal, if this is the same drug we've seen elsewhere, I'm not sure what could happen here," Morgan said tersely.

The marshal grunted toward Morgan. The two of them managed to pull Ivan to the aisle, fling him down on his front, where he was quickly pinned by the marshal's knee in his back.

"How the hell did you know what was happening all the way up here. I saw you from my seat near the back of the plane," Gillies asked, with confusion marking his face.

"I heard a weird sound, and I've been working the drug incidents that started here New Year's Eve, so I was tuned in," Morgan said, shrugging. She moved closer to Mike, grabbing onto the first aid kit a stewardess passed her. Mike was in rough shape, she noticed. His irises were black, his voice silent, and his body slack. "Marshal, what's the state of that kids' eyes? This one has no colour at all. Just black."

"This guy too," the Marshal said, "What's that mean?"

"It means this guy here could be at the same stage of drug reaction, but he hasn't reacted violently."

"Maybe having his arm chewed off stopped something," the marshal said as he picked Ivan up roughly from the floor.

"Be careful," Morgan said through gritted teeth, "he could go off again."

"I'm gonna need to talk to you before you get the next flight. Name's Gillies, Fred Gillies," the marshal said as he held onto the back of Ivan's neck and steered him toward the door and off the plane.

"Yeah, I figured," Morgan said. She looked again at Mike. "You okay, mister? You going off on me like your friend there?"

"N...no...no I am not okay. But I'm not crazy. What the fuck happened to him? He said he wanted more drugs, and he was hungry...a...and then went fuckin' nuts!"

"What kind of drugs did you both take?" Morgan asked. Her voice was stern, her face void of compassion for the bloodied man in front of her. "This is important. What did you take?"

"I...I dunno what it's called. I got 'em from a dealer at a party. Fun, or happy, or some shit like that."

"Joy?" Morgan shook him to make sure he heard her. "Is it called Joy? Where's the rest of it? In your hand luggage? Checked bag?" The airport police stomped on to the plane to remove Mike.

"It's hidden. In the lining of my suitcase and in my laptop. I can show you where."

She called Skelter before she was down the stairs outside the plane. "Skelter, we have a problem. Someone just had some kind of reaction on my plane...yes, I'm still in New York. We weren't off the ground. I'll meet you in the airport police offices here."

There was a commotion at the patrol car on the runway.

"Officers," Morgan said, her hands on her hips and her dark hair blowing across her eyebrows, "you can't put them in the same car. That guy there, in the backseat, was trying to eat this guy standing here."

She saw a smile momentarily cross Gillies' face before he returned it to neutral. "That's one way of describing it. Not sure that will make it into my report exactly."

"It should," she said. "It's going to be a frequent finding in the upcoming weeks, if the past few days are anything to go by."

Platt, Skelter, and Morgan sat with Marshal Gillies and the airport security director in a small office.

"I'm still at a loss as to how you knew what was going on at the front of the plane," Gillies said. His voice was deep, soft, and the smile that had briefly lit him up before was back. "Like, seriously, I had no idea there was anything happening up there."

"I noticed those two when I boarded, and thought there was something funny about them. I guess I was just tuned in to what was going on." It was Morgan's turn to keep her face poker straight, and she shrugged for added effect.

"It's just odd," Gillies said. "You were at the back of the plane, several rows behind me."

Morgan couldn't be sure if Gillies was impressed with her reaction, or mystified, but she was tired of his questions. "I have exceptional hearing, and I'm a good observer of human behaviour. I'm sure you are too. Anyway, it's time we get past my reaction and look at what we can find in their luggage. The guy who was attacked said it's in his suitcase lining."

While Skelter followed Gillies and the security director to where the suitcase and laptop would be examined, Platt and Morgan were left alone.

"You okay?" he asked, searching her eyes. He was seated on a rickety table that was pushed against the wall, at an angle that made him look ready for her to walk into his embrace.

Morgan stood in front of him. "I'm fine, though this isn't doing much for my dislike of flying."

"Want a hug?" he asked. His face, normally relaxed and with a ready grin, was serious. He held out his arms. She didn't hesitate.

"You feel warm and real," she said into his shoulder.

"I'm real. No zombies here." He tilted his head down and let her snuggle closer. "What do you want to do? It'll be a few hours before you can get another flight won't it?"

"I'm just waiting for James to call me with flight details." On cue, Morgan's phone buzzed and she looked at the screen. "It's James. Cross your fingers there's a flight today."

"There's a private flight but it doesn't leave New York until midnight. That okay?" James asked.

"Sounds fine," Morgan said, and then she looked at Platt, "Well Rob Platt, I'm here until midnight."

"Perfect," he said. "If you want, you could come see my place and we can check out the neighbourhood. Whaddya say?"

"Is it nearby?"

"Closer to work, but still in New York state," he smiled. "We'll make sure you're back here in plenty of time."

"Let's do it," she said, letting herself get lost in his dark brown eyes for a moment. "An unexpected chance to extend my time here in New York sounds like a really good thing."

"You sure? Because we had this no attachment thing and I can feel myself getting attached to you."

"You know what Rob? We work in dangerous situations all the time. Neither of us get any guarantees. Maybe we just need to seize the moments we get, and live life like there's no tomorrow."

They went looking for Skelter, who with some direction from Mike, had discovered the now familiar tear shaped vials of drugs. Mike had explained to Skelter that he wasn't a big drug user and had taken two hits of the drug, about four hours apart. Ivan, who had been placed under arrest and taken to hospital, had been more experimental and took twice as much in the same amount of time. The two men were cousins flying to England for a family funeral, and wanted the drugs to take the edge off things.

"Okay, I'm heading back to the office," Skelter said. "Who's coming with me?"

"How about a little detour, Skelter, and you drop me and Morgan off in my neighbourhood. She's here 'til midnight."

"Sure thing. I know you two are probably just dying to eat more pastrami."

"Jealous?" Morgan smiled.

"Not really. Platt, bring me one in the morning, alright? But don't tell my wife."

When Morgan boarded her flight that evening, she was happy to see that it was a small private jet, just as James had promised. There were five other passengers, and they were distributed throughout the plane so they didn't have to look or speak with each other. As the plane took off, Morgan leaned back against the headrest with her eyes closed while she replayed the afternoon in her mind.

After all the fuss was over at the La Guardia airport, Skelter had dropped Platt and Morgan off on a busy corner a couple of blocks from Platt's apartment on the West Side. It was a vibrant neighbourhood, and lively with traffic, people walking, and shops along the street. When they arrived at his apartment, Morgan had a yearning for having some space she could call her own once again. Rob lived in a well appointed building, and though the suite was small, there were tall windows letting in plenty of light, and it was close to work.

"And in-suite laundry," Platt said. "I know that may sound ridiculous, but I didn't want to have to manage life without it. This way if I have to jet off to work and there's laundry in the washer, it doesn't matter and I can just leave it."

"Just curious...what do you pay for a place like this here?" Morgan asked, taking in the sleeping area at the far end of the living space. It was a bachelor suite, but it was still a reasonable size.

"It's ridiculous what we pay here. This place is $3400 a month and I could never do it on a cop's salary, but I get a military pension on account of the leg and that helps. I don't need a car, because everything is close by." He shrugged. "It works."

"I had a great place with a nice view in Nova Scotia, and your place makes me miss it."

"The other attraction with this building is the monster sized gym. I can work out on my days off without having to leave home. What's your place like in London?"

Morgan gave a short laugh as she turned from the window. "I'm in a very small place, more like a dorm room. It's owned by the agency, and part of the war rooms that were set up during World War Two. Shared laundry," she said with a lopsided smile. "I haven't really been there much. I was going to try and find a small place to rent or maybe buy in the country so I could go do some writing or just escape the city on my day's off, but there hasn't been enough time to go find anything. Property is expensive there too."

"Do you think about moving back to Canada?"

"I'm not sure. I love Nova Scotia and I have a few friends there. Then again, winters are long and they can be dreary."

"I think Skelter and his wife like you. If you moved here, they're bound to have family dinners and invite you over."

"You mean you don't want to cook for me, and have me here with you?" she teased.

"Not until I get this robot leg of mine sorted out, at least. Besides, I thought we didn't have any attachment to each other, and it would be too much for me to assume," he said, pulling her close and kissing her forehead.

"We don't, but then again we do live dangerous lives and maybe, just maybe, that should count for something. I could come for a few weeks and help you after your surgery while I work on my book," she tipped her face up and kissed him.

"Hmm, what's this book about anyway?"

"It's a spy novel about a badass middle aged woman who likes to catch bad guys."

"You allowed to publish it?"

"You mean, will the agency let me publish it given that it might reveal secrets?"

"Yeah, that's what I mean."

"I haven't asked them. When I wrote it I was supposed to be retired, but then they invited me to come work for them in London, which turned into a stint here in New York."

"Did you change names and locations to protect the innocent, as it were?"

"I did indeed. But I think I have to rewrite some of it and position the main character as American or British. That way people won't be so inclined to think it's about me. And, apparently I need to do some rewriting for that happy ending if I want it to sell."

"You mentioned that. Why don't you want a happy ending?"

"Because my partner, like a lot of other people I have cared about, didn't make it."

"How did he die in real life? I heard from Skelter that your previous partner died on an op, but he didn't tell me much."

"Jake had a heart attack, on a boat, in the middle of a mission." She rubbed the back of her neck to relieve the tension that was building there.

"Oh shit, that's harsh. So, you put that ending in your book?" He didn't offer his condolences or say sorry, and Morgan was grateful for that.

"I wrote the book to show that despite the great connection the characters in the story had, there aren't too many spies who get a happy ending. You know, like Simon Templar and James Bond in the old spy novels. In those stories it was usually the girls who ended up dead, but in this case, it happened to be the guy." She paused. "Why does everyone think a book has to have a happy ending?" Her face was serious, and her brow furrowed as her eyes grew hard.

"I suppose it's just that most of them do, that's all. Bad guys get caught, people end up together despite obstacles, the prince finds the princess."

"Or maybe Cinderella turns out to be a real bitch and drives the prince crazy. There's more than one possible ending to a story, Rob." She was getting upset thinking about her agent pressuring her to rewrite the end of her book. *Let it go, Morgan, just let it go. Enjoy the afternoon.*

"Yeah, I suppose there is. I just never thought about it." He changed the topic slightly. "I *was* thinking about taking Skelter up on his offer to join him at the FBI, or your suggestion to work with ACTI. But judging by the death rate in both those jobs, maybe I'll have a longer life expectancy if I keep working as a New York City cop."

"Ha. I didn't know you were seriously thinking about changing teams."

"I'll have you know that I do a lot of thinking. Of course, right now I'm considering whether we go out for lunch, or stay here and work up an appetite, then go out later."

Morgan smiled to herself as the plane taxied along the runway, thinking back to Rob's kisses and his touch, briefly reliving an afternoon of lovemaking and conversation that left just barely enough time to hop into a cab and get to the airport.

Chapter Six

London

"Welcome back, Morgan!" James called out from his position over the digital table where he performed his magic. "We've missed you!"

"Liar," Morgan said, looking over at her cousin. She had entered the ACTI office area before returning to her room, feeling refreshed after sleeping on the plane and coming straight from the airport. With the time change, it was only 0800 in New York, but now here she was in London where it was noon and the day was well underway.

"Hello, Director Winfeld," a calm, female voice addressed her from across the room. The woman was in her early thirties, platinum blonde expensive hair coiffed into a modern French twist, high buttoned white blouse tucked into a grey pencil skirt perfectly hemmed at the knee.

A new psychologist. Great.

Morgan turned to James, "Where'd doctor whatshername go? Who is this?"

"This is Dr. Meriweather," James said as an introduction. "Dr. Meriweather, meet Morgan Winfeld, our Assistant Director of Field Operations."

The doctor stuck out her hand and crossed the room quickly, the click, click, click of her four inch heels making Morgan look down at the woman's stunning, but impractical, shoes. Morgan returned the handshake lightly, so she wouldn't knock the doctor off her impractical footwear.

"Our previous psychologist moved on to a similar job with the London Police. Dr Meriweather here has experience working with emergency responders and military vets with post traumatic stress injuries," James offered.

"When did you start here, Doctor?" Morgan tried to make her voice sound welcoming, instead of having it betray annoyance. Breaking in a new psychologist wasn't something she wanted to do just now.

"Right after the holidays. Why?"

"Are you up to speed on the work we were doing in New York? If not, James can catch you up. I need to see Director Mullins in about fifteen minutes, and if you want you can join us." *Let's see if you are a little stronger than your predecessor, because you are going to need to be if you're going to help this team in the fallout once it gets to England.*

"Um, her security clearance isn't all finished yet," James said. "Not sure she can meet with you and the director for this." He looked at Dr. Meriweather with a shrug and said, "Sorry Doc."

"It's alright," she said. "I'm sure it'll be here soon. I don't know what the hold up is." She picked at a non-existent piece of lint on her tailored skirt.

"Well, never mind, I'll go and see him. I guess we will catch you up later," Morgan said. "James, you should join me if you're available."

"Me?" James hesitated. "You've never invited me before."

"Doesn't mean you shouldn't be invited today. Mullins' office, ten minutes."

"Good," he said. "I'll grab coffees, then, shall I?"

"I'll give you twenty minutes if you are bringing coffee." She raised an eyebrow and tilted her head slightly, "And thank you, because coffee would be nice."

Morgan stopped in a small washroom on her way to Director Mullins' office. In her weeks away in New York, there had been no acknowledgements nor need for rank and she had almost forgotten about the promotion to assistant director before she'd left. She ran the water into the tiny sink for a moment, and watched the water droplets as they hit the porcelain and splashed onto the side of the basin as though trying to escape.

You can't get away, little water droplets. It's all hands on deck for this, and no one is going to be slacking off. Morgan rinsed her face, trying to clear the seven hours of plane travel and make herself look like an assistant director. She adjusted her leather jacket so it sat properly across her hips, then gave up trying to look put together like the fine Dr. Meriweather, and waltzed into Director Mullins' office.

"Welcome back, Winfeld," he said cheerfully. "Shall we meet in your office instead of here? I believe everything is set up for you."

The news of an office surprised Morgan. "Pardon?"

"All directors of the agency have an office. Come, come, you're just two doors down the hall from here," Mullins smiled as he stood and indicated the door.

There was a small sign with 'M Winfeld Director, Field Ops' on the door. Morgan looked around the room and nodded. "Nice," she said. "Thank you, but I thought I was an Assistant Director."

"Your work in New York just got you promoted. Congratulations," Mullins said without fanfare.

Inside was a multifunction desk with a computer, a brand new adjustable chair, and beside it a round meeting table with four acrylic molded chairs. Under the small window was a wide bookcase that was empty of books, but expectant looking. On the middle of the meeting table sat a bottle of scotch beside a small vase with a bunch of daisies in it. There was a door connecting the office to a room next door.

"Your assistant will be through the door there. You get to pick who you want from the staff pool, or if you're in less of a hurry you can hire someone."

"An assistant? Who has assistants anymore? I wouldn't even know how to start with one."

"All the directors get one, and they are part secretary, part organizer, and available to you whatever hours you agree on. Everyone at our level has someone here, Morgan."

"Our level. Right. We are both at the same level now. So, who am I reporting to?" Morgan stood, unsure of whether to sit or find a glass for some scotch.

"You'll report to Chief Commander Steeves, same as I do, and I can help you through the first days as you settle in. You've got twelve field agents on your team to look after, and six of them are deployed in various places right now."

"So what are you going to be doing, Mullins? You're currently looking after those agents, aren't you?"

"I am, but not in a way that the agency needs apparently. I am going to Australia as the southern hemisphere coordinator in recognition for my hard work." He stood close to the window, but as a seasoned operative he avoided being in front of it. His face was miserable and tormented.

"You're lucky then," Morgan said, "The *Joy19* issue hasn't made it to Oz yet," she said sincerely.

"Lucky? I'm not lucky. Do you have any idea how hard I've worked to get this position, and now they are shuffling me off? My wife is livid. The kids are refusing to come and they are in their teens so it looks like I am leaving here for two years and I'll be alone on a bloody colony."

"A colony? You know we don't call them that nowadays, right Mullins? You do remember that I am from one of those countries you refer to as a 'colony' don't you?"

"Yes, er, of course I do. That's not really what I meant." He was backtracking, and not wanting to stop him from putting his foot in his mouth, Morgan sat quietly in the office chair at her desk.

"Sorry," Mullins said after a pregnant pause. "The news took me by surprise and I'm still getting used to it."

"Do some research, and then you'll know what you're getting into. Australia is amazing, plus it's close to all those other places and you can do some travelling, have some fun. Maybe it's not the punishment you think it is. Now, on to other things you mentioned, like having an assistant. Are the candidates in our hiring pool able to do research? And are they highly skilled and good with tech?"

"They might be," Mullins said, sitting down and crossing his right ankle over his left knee. "Do you need some research done?"

"Possibly. Are you up to date on this drug case I was working on in New York? Do you know the problem is international?"

"Shamefully, I must say no. I believe Chief Commander Steeves might be on top of it. I took some time off over the holidays, and he was looking after my workload. I got back to work today."

James entered the room with a tray of coffee, and behind him was a woman with a plate of cookies. Morgan frowned at James.

"Morgan, this is Natalie. She wants to be your assistant, so let me introduce you." He turned to Natalie and said, "Natalie, this is Morgan Winfeld."

"This seems an odd time and place for an interview," Morgan said, picking up a chocolate digestive from the plate Natalie held, "but you have good taste in cookies. Explain yourself Natalie."

Natalie was ready for Morgan's direct questions, no doubt having been briefed by James.

"Ma'am, my name is Natalie Wooden. I have a degree in library studies, and..."

Morgan cut the young woman off. "So you're a researcher?"

"Oh yes ma'am, a researcher, academic writer, and I'm good with digital technology, too. I'm currently working part-time on a graduate degree in communications."

"Go on," Morgan invited, gesturing to everyone to seat themselves around the table. There was a pause in Natalie's presentation while they all got settled. "And please stop calling me ma'am."

"S...sorry, Director Winfeld," the woman said hesitantly.

Morgan rolled her eyes.

"Morgan?" Natalie asked with a question mark on her face.

"Please," Morgan replied. "I know there are loads of titles here and rank, but you can skip that as long as you have cookies all the time. Go ahead."

"Okay, and I will try and remember to you call them cookies since we call them biscuits here. When I heard you were in New York after your promotion to assistant director, I hoped there was a chance for me to continue learning here and get myself ready to apply for a job on your team. I was hoping to meet with you as soon as you returned, and I honestly am sorry that it happened to be within thirty minutes of you getting back to the office, but I think I can help. I have a flare for electronics and digital technology, I mentioned I'm good at research, and I've been here for two years now so I know my way around the agency."

"Impressive," Morgan said. *If this Joy19 issue continues much longer, in addition to the cyber crimes file, I am going to need some extra help and obviously James can't do it all. Not that I need a partner per se in this role, but if I am splitting my time between being a director and sometimes being in the field or sometimes being abroad, she could make life a little easier.* She looked at Director Mullins. "You can vouch for her?"

"Yes," he said. "She's got an entirely unblemished record and top secret, codeword, special access...she's the real deal."

"And you, James, you can vouch for her?"

"Yeah," he said, blushing ever so slightly. "We went to school together. She's a smart person, someone we need."

Are we related? Morgan pushed the thought to James, not expecting a reaction but more because she was asking herself. James looked at her sharply, then gave a half shake of his head to indicate no, but he said nothing. *Oh my god, that worked. You heard what I said.* James gave a full nod as he picked up his coffee so the others wouldn't notice.

Morgan paused as the realization that not only could she hear conversations at ridiculous distances, but she just exchanged thoughts with James. She paused a moment to collect herself and said, "Good then, you've got the recommendations and the security clearance. You're in! Welcome to the team. This *Joy19* case is a doozy."

"Before we start on that," Mullins said holding up his hand, "Shall we bring Dr. Meriweather in on this? As the psychologist we may need her, and frankly, she's going to have to debrief you now that you're back, Morgan."

"She apparently lacks a security clearance and as such we can't let her know what we discuss here," Morgan said.

"Seriously?" Mullins said. "What's the hold up? Normally no one starts here without that."

Natalie jumped into the conversation. "If I might, Sir, I have been working in human resources and I can answer this for you. The hold up is because of positive findings in her security review. She has a drug trafficking conviction."

"She's a drug addict." Morgan stated it as a fact rather than asking a question.

"No ma'am...er, Morgan. Not that we know of, anyway. She passed her physical screenings, so if she was on something we would have picked that up. She was arrested for trying to bring drugs back from abroad for the purpose of trafficking while she was on a vacation a few year's ago." Natalie spoke clearly, and quickly. She ended her sentences with a bob to her head as if to emphasize the importance of the details.

Morgan said slowly. "How the *hell* did she get through the hiring process?"

"Not that it's an excuse but we were in a hurry to hire someone and were asked to do some things out of order. She changed her name when she got married and so we dropped the ball on her record right up until we ran her fingerprints on her first day at work," Natalie said.

"So she was deliberately trying to hide the conviction from us? She didn't disclose it on her application?" Morgan asked.

"Right, but she passed every element in the process. It seems she was trying to prove she could be valuable first, so that we might ignore the conviction," Natalie said.

The room went quiet for a moment and Morgan spoke to shatter the awkward silence that was growing. "I hope you all see the irony in this. We're a spy agency and supposed to be really good at stuff, and instead we just let the proverbial wolf in through the front fucking door."

Director Mullins tapped his fingers on the table. "She also passed the lie detector test. This won't do. It won't do at all. We cannot offer a security clearance to someone with a conviction like that, and we will have a damned hard time letting her go quietly given we already hired her and gave her access to our building, and staff."

"Let me talk to her and see what I can find out. We'll see if she is gearing up to do some good by working with the agency, or to cause havoc," Morgan said.

She briefed the group on what had happened in New York, including a recap of the six weeks when she and Skelter were working on the cyber crime file. The interruption to their work because of *Joy19* was no small matter. She told the group about several locations – including England, Scotland, and Ireland, where *Joy19* issues were reported in the last few days. She also spoke directly and unemotionally about her concerns of vigilante style enforcement that might see innocent people, including children, getting murdered because they "might" be part of the drug establishment, but also those who might not be and could be swept along in a convenient effort to eliminate trouble that didn't even exist.

Two hours later, the meeting was over and Morgan sat at her desk for a moment gathering her thoughts. A knock at the door broke her reverie, and Chief Commander Steeves popped his head in. "Welcome back," he said. "It's good to see you, and if you need anything, holler.

Also, we are planning a late Christmas party at my place a week from Saturday since you missed the entire season. You'll be there of course, but I need to know if you are bringing a date so I have enough napkins."

"No date, I'll bring napkins if you want."

"A week from Saturday, 2000 hours, don't be late."

"Why do people here start parties so late in the day?" she asked.

He left, and Morgan smiled to herself over the way he had shared the invitation. It was just like him. No options, because if he had given her one she would have begged off and made an excuse about not having time to celebrate.

Morgan was about to test the intercom on her desk that connected her to Natalie, then decided against it. She picked up her phone and texted instead.

Hey Nat, please see what you
can arrange for office supplies.
There aren't any in here.

Natalie quickly replied:

Aren't we doing most things
digitally? What supplies would you need?

Morgan looked at the message and smiled. This was going to be fun.

I have 3 empty drawers in
this desk and they sound
hollow. They need stuff in
them to dampen the noise.

I can pick up some pictures for your

walls to dampen the sound. What do you like?

Castles and ancient battlements.
But I still need stuff for the
drawers in this desk.

You could lock your firearm in one of them.

My firearm stays attached to
my body. You need to know this
in case you ever plan a sneak
attack.

But you won't need it working in the office,
will you?

It keeps me company okay?
How about a pack of sticky
notes and a box of pens?

Pens? Really? You don't have a pen?

No, I don't. No stapler either
but there is an in-and-out tray here
that is crying to be meaningful.

I'm in the process of scanning and digitizing
papers. It's a lot easier to do if they aren't stapled.

Okay, then I need some glasses for this scotch
& an umbrella to keep in these drawers.

There are umbrellas available at the entrance to our building. You take one when you leave, and put it back when you return.

I thought you were supposed to be assisting me in doing my job.

I am. I just helped you avoid cluttering up a perfectly good office.

Oh. Roger that.

Morgan smiled as she put her phone in the front pocket of her jeans and left her office. The exchange with Nat had been fun, but she needed to see Meriweather.

"Dr. Meriweather, do you have a minute?" Morgan announced at the psychologist's door.

"Yes, I do. I need to get your debriefing done but apparently I can't because of this security clearance issue."

"I can't help you with my debrief, because things are classified," Morgan said crisply, "but I do need to ask you some questions about your security clearance. For instance, why didn't you tell us about the drug conviction when you applied here? There's a box in the application screen that you had to answer, where you deliberately clicked on the wrong box and lied."

"Well, I thought...I thought if I left that until later, maybe I would at least get to the interview stage and then, you know...beg for forgiveness." She smiled weakly. Morgan remained unimpressed.

"It seems like you were testing us to see if we could catch you, and then you might ask for forgiveness if forced to, but only if you were pushed to it. Is that right?"

"Well yes, but then as I got through the interviews and psych assessment, and all the hoops, I thought perhaps no one had figured it out...and...," she shrugged.

"And so you expected to come to work somewhere that deals in international secrets but wouldn't catch you in a lie?"

"W...what do you mean?"

"You think we are foolish enough to let you in here? C'mon, Meriweather. What's the deal with you?"

Meriweather had the good sense to look uncomfortable. She got up from her chair and started pacing in front of the window, her arms crossed, her brow creased.

Morgan wondered if she could read any of the doctor's thoughts. She wasn't sure if she could probe outside her family, and wasn't sure she wanted to try it on someone new just now, since it could mean Meriweather would, in turn, know she was being read.

Aw fuck it. I won't know if I don't try. Morgan adjusted herself in the chair. She looked at the doctor, and breathed deeply, focusing on the doctor's face, which was warping itself into an even deeper frown.

"I don't know what to tell you," Meriweather said. "I'm sure you've seen the arrest reports. I served my sentence and finished university. I'm qualified for this position."

Morgan let the words hang in the air as Meriweather's thoughts continued and went straight into Morgan's head.

"I can't stop working here. I can't let this woman kick me out. My boss will kill me if I eff this up." Meriweather thought. Then she thought something in Cantonese and Morgan sat up straight as she realized Meriweather was working for the Chinese.

A trained Chinese operative could probably beat a lie detector test. Some of this was starting to make sense. Morgan paused so she could choose her words carefully in order to get more out of Meriweather before the doctor figured out her mind was being read.

"What on earth would make you think you could get a job here with that kind of a conviction? And how is it you managed to get your qualifications as a psychologist in England? That's tough to get for someone with a criminal record, isn't it?"

"I passed all the exams, that's how I got it!"

"You must have lied to the psychologist's association about the conviction, obviously, because you could not have passed the board scrutiny if you had admitted it."

"I could and I did pass the scrutiny...," Meriweather said as her eyes narrowed.

"But only because you lied. I'm going to make a couple of calls. What university did you attend?"

"Cambridge."

"Okay, and what name did you use there?"

Meriweather sighed and sat down hard in her chair. She continued thinking in Chinese, but Morgan couldn't make it out.

"My last name was Lee. My birth name is Jacinda Lee."

"And?"

Meriweather looked at Morgan and the doctor's eyes went hard. Her hair was starting to escape in wisps from her bun as her frustration and embarrassment grew.

"And I was born in China to British parents who lived in Hong Kong."

"So, you're not telling me, but you are a Chinese operative."

"I didn't say that."

"You didn't have to." Morgan said. "You and I are finished here."

"You...you mean I am free to go?"

Morgan laughed. "Free? No, you're not free. You lied to get a job here, and to get your psychologist's license. I can assure you that you're going to be lost in paperwork hell before you are deported to China, if ACTI will even let you go."

"Deported? But why? I served my time for the drug conviction. I am a British citizen."

"You might think you're British, but as a Chinese operative trying to spy on us, you're a traitor. You are not welcome here Dr. Meriweather."

Morgan could hear Meriweather's thoughts easily as the young woman became more agitated.

"Don't think about leaving," Morgan said. "There's nowhere you could go right now that you can't be found."

Meriweather came around the desk, ready to take a run at Morgan and escape.

"Sit," Morgan commanded, "if you know what's good for you."

"Those fingerprints of mine were supposed to be changed on all the official records. You weren't supposed to find out who I am. I'm not going to stay here and put up with your interrogation. I'm leaving." Meriweather drew herself up to her full height.

"You are imposing in those high heels. But you aren't going anywhere." Morgan said as she slowly stood up.

Meriweather pulled a long pin from her carefully coiffed hair and held it in front of her, threatening to stab Morgan. The dagger was at least three inches long, and Morgan wondered if it could be poisoned. *Not exactly what I imagined today,* she thought.

Morgan positioned herself in a wide stance, while her right hand reached across her body for the gun in her holster. "There's no need for you to go anywhere, and I am a really good shot," Morgan said as she pointed the gun at Meriweather. "Not that I want to kill you, because I think people are going to want to ask you lots of questions."

Meriweather didn't hesitate. She moved forward at Morgan. Morgan fired into Meriweather's lower left leg, and the woman crumpled, still holding the nasty hairpin toward Morgan defensively. Morgan kicked the woman's hand with a booted foot, and the hairpin flew across the room.

Morgan pulled out her phone to call the security detail, when James opened the door.

"I've called security and they are right behind me," he said.

"She'll need a doctor first. Be careful, she's feisty," Morgan said, then looked at James, "I was about to call you when you arrived at the door."

"I know," he smiled. "I have this room bugged since the doctor wasn't through scrutiny yet, so I knew what was going on."

Meriweather rolled her eyes and groaned. "I am so screwed," she said.

"Not yet, but you're going to wish you had it so easy," Morgan said as she picked up the hairpin and looked at it closely. "James, we should get this analyzed."

Chapter Seven

A couple of hours later, with Meriweather's leg bandaged and questioning ready to begin, Morgan went to visit James. "Any news?" she said, approaching him as he stood at his tabletop computer, the screen in front of him a mass of colour and movement as he conducted his research.

"More *Joy19* incidents are taking place all over, Morgan. It's not looking good."

"We've got to stop this drug from spreading, and we need to stop people getting killed who may or may not have ingested it."

"I've got a map to show you reported incidents," he said. His tabletop responded to some quick tapping by displaying a map of the world, with red pinpoints on it. "Those red pins are reported incidents of *Joy19* reactions."

"Looks like it's been a busy day," Morgan said as more red dots came on the map with each thirty second refresh of the screen.

"I can add a blue dot for military and police response," James said, fingers flying on the keyboard.

Morgan looked at the table as the pins appeared. She walked around to stand opposite from James and bent down slightly to view things from an angle. She didn't speak for several moments, just watched the pins, moved a few steps, and watched the pins again. The map looked like one of the images of earth taken from space at nighttime, where the lights were intense near big cities, and then spread out and turned into nothing in rural areas. Except that the lights were red dots showing *Joy19* spreading across the U.S. to some degree or another, and western Europe was the same.

"So there are definitely more activities taking place around the United States, but Europe is not far behind. I'm not seeing anything in Australia and Africa. What about Eastern Europe?" Morgan's brows were tightly furrowed.

"Some of those places we just don't have much intel about. Australia, however, does not seem to be infected. Because of the time and distance from the U.S., the Aussie's were able to implement protocols and stop much of what was trying to get into the country, so far as we're able to tell. Same for New Zealand. We know some areas of Africa have issues from the chatter we can pick up, but it's spotty. For sure there have been reactions in Egypt and South Africa, but there's not much reporting elsewhere, just scuttlebutt."

"I need to meet with the other directors, and we are going to have to find a new doc."

"I'll see what human resources can do."

"Great. Also, I'd like you to be at the meeting. Be prepared to share that screen with all the pins on it. Later, we should really figure out this thing with me being able to push my questions to you without opening my mouth, and how you were able to answer me."

"Yeah, about that. You know I don't have any extra sensory powers, right? It's something I'm keenly aware of because it made me stand out as weird within my own family, so I don't understand it either. Are you reading my thoughts right now?"

"Nope, I was trying earlier but stopped, because I don't really want to know when you are thinking about things unrelated to work. It's rattling me because I could read Meriweather's thoughts and I don't think she's related to us. Let's keep it to ourselves for now, and talk about it later."

Morgan left James and then called Skelter in New York. "I'm hopeful you have some news on an antidote for *Joy19*," she said.

"I'm well," Skelter replied curtly. "Thank you for asking."

She could hear him tapping his pen on the edge of a desk in an irritated manner. "Sorry, Skelter. I was engrossed in something here and forgot how much you like chit chat. How are you? How's the wife and kids?"

"We're good, thanks for asking. I wish you were still here, because things are going haywire. Now, tell me what you need?"

"Any news on an antidote yet? Where are we at with that?"

"Well, we aren't anywhere. Apparently, it can take years to develop something, and they are telling me they don't have anything useful yet."

"Shit. Have you seen the incident maps?"

"Yeah, James sent them to me. It's getting worse here, Morgan. We've got people out on the street having reactions. They aren't in hiding in someone's basement or at a party. They're out in public."

"What about public service announcements? You got them off the ground there ahead of anyone else. Are they helping?"

"Not yet. I'm not even sure we are hitting the right audience."

"Are you targeting social media?"

"Only barely. Mostly, it's radio and TV ads, and we're sharing them in a restricted manner online."

"Restricted by what?"

"Money for ads, mostly. The rate these companies want to charge for us to use their platforms is outta sight and I still don't have a budget approved."

"Seriously? Has anyone approached the advertisers individually?"

"I wouldn't even know how to start."

"I do. I'll call you back." She disconnected without saying goodbye and marched into Mullins' office. "Director, we need a sitrep meeting here, but before that I need you to give me the contact information for the head of each of the social networks as well as the big search engines."

"Okay, I'll be at the meeting, but I don't have those peoples' contact info," Mullins lied smoothly. *Besides, if I'm about to get screwed out of my career, I'll take anyone I can out with me.*

Morgan registered the thoughts that Mullin was working through and decided to circumvent his pettiness and work on her assertive director approach instead. "Yes, you do. Don't try lying to me Mullins because I'm a human bullshit detector. You were at the privacy commission hearings into activity of all those companies, and I remember seeing you in pictures during the deposition given by the social media guy ... I can't think of his name right now, but it's the guy who always wears t-shirts and jeans. I think he would help us."

"He would?"

"Well, if he doesn't and this thing doesn't stop, there's a good chance he's going to lose a huge majority of advertisers that fund his company through ad revenue, or their customers."

"He is?"

"Yup."

"How do you know that?"

"Because I've been working with Skelter for weeks now, and he's an optimist. It must be rubbing off."

"Have you thought of t-shirt man's name yet?" Mullins said trying not to laugh.

"Nope, don't need to until I call him," Morgan said.

Mullins looked up a number on his phone and texted it to Morgan. "Oh, and his wife's number is here too. One or the other will be a good place to start."

Morgan didn't wait. She tapped the first phone number. Reaching voicemail, she left a vague message and then called his wife. More voicemail.

"How about the search engine guy?"

"I don't have that one."

"Alright, I'm going to enlist James."

"What makes you think any of these people will help us?"

"They got into so much trouble over privacy issues, illegal eavesdropping, and data collection over the last few years that it's staggering. These companies love ones and zeroes, Mullins. Gatherers of information, with exceptional capability for sending outgoing messaging, too. They aren't going to help us because they're humanitarians, they're going to do it because they need to preserve the hold they have on all that data. I'm going to lean on them and let them know how good this could be for their bottom line. Plus, I heard somewhere that the guy who invented the internet is devastated over how it's been used. That should give us some more leverage."

As she left Mullins' office, Morgan spotted Natalie just outside her office.

"Nat, I need your help."

"Oh good."

"Is it okay for me to call you Nat, or not?"

"I like the way you say it, so it's a good thing," Nat said with a bob of her head.

"Look, I know you are excited about your new position and I should be doing some kind of 'onboarding' stuff with you, but I don't even understand the scope of your job yet. In the meantime, I have a problem and I need you to work with James and track down some people."

"Sure, Morgan that's not hard for me to do. And don't worry about the orientation stuff. I know we are working this out as we go. Now, who are we looking for?"

"The guy who created the internet, he's English if I remember rightly, so hopefully he's not far from here. And I have a phone number for the head of the world's biggest social media company, but he isn't taking my calls. I'll need you to work on that, too."

"On it."

Thirty minutes later, Morgan was wrapping up the sitrep meeting when Natalie knocked gently on the door.

"Enter," Morgan said.

"Ma'am, I mean Morgan, I have booked a dinner meeting for you this evening with Henry Bergman, the founder of the world wide web. He is teaching at Oxford today, and will be home for dinner with his wife at 1900 hours. You and James are expected."

"Me and James, Nat?"

"I figured it would give you and James a chance to talk about a couple of outstanding things, plus James is the tech lead for the team, and Professor Bergman might need him to provide some technical details."

"Well done Nat, thank you."

"It's a couple of hours from here Morgan, depending on traffic, so you'll need to leave straightaway."

"Let James know I can be ready to leave here in ten minutes. We'll need a car."

"Certainly."

As she pulled up outside Professor Bergman's house, Morgan nodded appreciatively. "It's just what I'd expect a university professor to live in, though not necessarily the guy who invented the internet."

"You know he didn't do it singlehandedly, don't you?" James said as they got out of the car.

"Yeah, sure," Morgan said smoothly.

"Liar," he laughed.

As they approached the oversized front door, Morgan could hear voices from inside. She cocked her head slightly and motioned to James to stop and wait a moment.

"You invited strangers here to dinner?" A deep male voice said from inside the house.

"The woman said it was a matter of grave importance, and that you were needed on priority."

"But you don't like having people to dinner. Are you alright with this?"

"Of course, darling, maybe a little excitement is just what we need around here."

Morgan lightly rapped on the oversized door with a brass lion's head, and the door opened almost immediately.

"Hullo," the man said cheerfully. "You must be Morgan, come in. And James."

Beside him in a wheelchair, a woman sat straight and tall. She pushed the hair back from her face with a trembling hand.

He's protecting her. Not surprising given the wheelchair, Morgan thought.

"Thank you for meeting with us on such short notice. I really appreciate it. The invitation to dinner was very kind." Morgan said. She offered a bottle of scotch to the professor, who took it and smiled.

"You acting types do like the good stuff," he said.

"Acting types, Professor?" Morgan said, eyebrows raised and a look of confusion making the light creases stand out on her brow more than usual.

"Yes, your assistant said to my wife that you were coming here to ask about my help with an acting troupe. Is that not correct?"

"I am a bit hard of hearing," Deidre said and then she held up a sign that said, 'Dining room is secure we can talk there' and, pressing the joystick lever at her right hand, she led the way across a marble foyer and into a massive dining room.

"Your home is stunning," Morgan said sincerely.

"It's old and full of character. It's my favourite place in the world," Deidre said. "C.S. Lewis lived here for about thirty years, and it's supposed to be a residence for the university and also host museum style tours. We were able to lease it because the foundation has had so much trouble raising money. With luck, it'll stay that way until Henry retires."

"When is Henry planning to retire?" Morgan asked, looking at them both with curiosity.

"I'm on the freedom-seventy-five plan," Henry laughed. "I know, people are surprised to hear that. They think I must have made a mint at the world wide web, and as a treasured lecturer here at Oxford as well as sometimes visiting M.I.T. But real life doesn't work that way. So, seventy-five it is, a little more than ten years, as long as I can still get to classes from here."

James pulled a scrambler from his backpack and set it on the table near the window. "If you don't mind Professor, this is turned on and will stop anyone who might be curious from hearing us. Each time we get a smarter piece of kit, someone tries to make something better in response, but this has proved very effective for us."

"Well, leave it on then," the professor said. "We regularly check the entire house, but this room has had some very special treatment, as has my study, so you shouldn't have to worry. Hopefully my own security measures explains our charade about the acting troupe at the front door just now. Entrances and exits are vulnerable spots, as you can imagine."

"Dinner will be ready in twenty minutes or so," Deidre offered. "If you want to chit chat, that's fine, or perhaps if you'd rather, you can discuss the matter you are here for and then enjoy your meal afterward."

"I'm happy to get right down to business if that's preferred," Morgan said. "That way, if I manage to annoy anyone, you can ask us to leave and we won't have to disturb your dinner." Morgan's smile was tense.

Deidre laughed. "Oh my dear, that will never happen. It's been ages since Henry had covert stuff going on. This is terrifying and fun."

James looked at Deidre and then to the professor, "Can I help do anything for dinner? Do you need any help in the kitchen?"

"That's kind of you, James. As you can imagine, Deidre isn't cooking much these days. Since her multiple sclerosis got bad, she's been confined to that chair and we hired a cook and a housekeeper."

Deidre leaned in to whisper, "Pretty sure even if I got better, I'd keep the staff. I have become accustomed to signing cheques instead of standing at the sink."

Deidre excused herself to check on dinner and Morgan gratefully accepted a scotch the professor poured from his collection. James joined her, and made a face as the nectar reached his palate.

"Sir, I don't know if you've heard about the outbreak of drug reactions since New Year. They started in New York, but are spreading around the world."

"Call me Henry. Yes, I heard. There have been incidents at a few British universities that I know of, but so far nothing at Oxford, thank God."

"Are you religious, Sir?" James asked casually, taking a sip of water. "I noticed lots of scientific decoration here, and history, but nothing religious."

"Hell no, just seemed like a good way to end that sentence," the professor laughed. "You need humour when discussing zombies, right?"

The conversation flowed easily, and Morgan used Deidre's polite absence to bring the professor up to date. "We are really concerned about how this drug reaction can turn into a political war, like the cold war but much worse with the potential numbers of people who could be killed, if you can imagine. I read in an article how disappointed you are that the internet has turned into something it was never intended and I thought perhaps we could leverage how you feel about it into some help. We would like to speak with the leaders of social media networks and the big search engines, so we can develop some public announcements to interfere with the spread of the drugs, and perhaps get some better intel than we have right now."

"You know I'd like to help, or you wouldn't be here. You're right that the internet and the web have been used for things never intended. But if I give you access to the data that gets collected, you could use it just as nefariously as a government who could be responsible for this kind of drug war you speak of."

"I know, Henry. It's a double edged sword. But if we can't get a handle on this, there's no telling how many people are going to die."

"But in this age, why wouldn't you simply try to retaliate in kind if you have the data we can give you?"

Morgan paused and then jumped back in, "I realize what you're saying is it's best if you don't help at all if there's no way to know who you're helping." *But that's not the way to stop this!* She felt bile rising in her throat at the potential for help slipping away.

"One second, what did you say there at the end?" the professor asked quietly.

"Er, it's best if you don't help at all if there's no way to know who you're helping?"

"No, after that, you said something but your lips weren't moving."

Morgan looked at him and blinked, giving her thoughts a moment to catch up with what he was saying.

Try it again, Morgan heard in the professor's voice in her head. *Go on.*

Morgan looked at James. He shrugged unhelpfully.

Morgan turned her attention to the professor. She sent a little push along with the thought, *Can you hear me Henry?*

Yes, she heard back in Henry's voice. *And I believe James can hear this also.*

James nodded, his eyes wide.

Morgan looked directly at the professor. *We are on a mission to stop mass extinction of potentially hundreds of thousands of people. And, we know law enforcers are ready to do their jobs and try to stop it, but we are worried that vigilantes or mercenaries could also be used. If they let loose on refugee camps, or border lockdowns in the U.S. to stop Mexican and South American refugees, well, we could be talking about millions of people, murdered.*

"Hmm. Well, I can arrange a discussion for you with whomever you'd like, but I don't think they'll be open to letting you access their data," Henry said aloud.

"A conversation would help," Morgan said. "It's a start. We don't have to talk about the data if they will help us, but it's bound to come up. We are certain that whomever is behind this is working with a treasure trove of data; their infiltration has been incredible. That also means they've got money, and international agents who are working for them. We need to issue worldwide messaging about the danger of these drugs. Messages aimed at users, street level drug pushers, and the entire hierarchy. We've got to blanket the web, including every corner, dark channel, whatever."

"Dinner is served," Deidre said from the doorway. "Let's eat."

"I'm starving," James said, moving toward the table.

"I'm definitely going to help with the public messaging. This is something I can assist with, possibly more than you can imagine," Henry said, as he took his seat at the ornately carved wooden table.

"It needs to go worldwide, in multiple languages, and to be culturally appropriate," Morgan said, taking a seat. She glanced at the array of cutlery and hoped she would be able to work out what to use.

"Naturally," the professor replied. "Count me onboard and I'll connect with my counterparts to get their support, as a start."

"We have a multi-disciplinary team available in the U.S. I was there working with them when this all first got started," Morgan said. Out of respect for Deidre, Morgan switched to more banal topics, and the meal proceeded.

"That was delicious," Morgan said afterward. "Please compliment your chef, and ask if he'll deliver the occasional meal to London."

"You'll be here from time to time in the next while, I am sure," Deidre said nodding her head emphatically. "And you are welcome anytime. We have several guest rooms here, and there is even a cottage on the property, a converted garage that we intended to rent out, but could never get our potential renters approved by our security detail. You'd probably be approved, though," she said with a smile.

"A cottage? Really?" asked Morgan. "I've been looking for a place where I could put my feet up on my days off. I'd love to look at it sometime."

Deidre said, "Once I first moved into the wheelchair, I became uncomfortable with entertaining. But now that we have so much help, I feel like I am up for anything."

"I, for one, don't mind coming to visit if there are meals involved," James said. "I'm always ready to eat."

"I never thought to ask you James, what have you been eating since you got to London?" Morgan asked.

"I have become part of the takeaway set," he laughed. His freckled face crinkled, and his eyes smiled. "Every corner in the city has a takeaway of some kind; cheap food, convenient, not that healthy. But now that's out in the open, I think we could all benefit from having a chef around the office."

They shared a laugh, the tension that had risen over the drug discussion dispelled by talk of food and relaxation. "Henry can take you out to the cottage after dinner," Deidre said. "He checks the fence line every night and just loves to zoom around on his little golf cart." She smiled at her husband.

"It's not a little golf cart," Henry said chuckling and looking at his wife with love. "It's a modified lawn tractor. It'll do thirty miles per hour if you let it, and it's been a godsend with this bumpy terrain."

After dinner, Morgan followed Henry out to his lawn tractor.

"It's only 300 yards from here to the cottage, it's a converted studio that was originally a kiln," Henry said. "Just far enough with this chill that I'd rather drive than walk. Does that suit you?"

"Yes, that sounds just fine," Morgan said as she climbed into the seat beside him. They drove along a path that had been smooth asphalt at one time, but was now heaved and cracked at regular intervals. First, they looked at the fence line, which was an immaculately trimmed hedge.

"I see what you mean about bumpy!" Morgan said, "but this place is beautiful. How much security do you have with all these hedges as opposed to fencing?"

"We've been here five years, and as a computer scientist, I've spent many hours putting wiring, cameras, and all kinds of goodies around the perimeter and inside. I love it here, as does Deidre. We have everything we need nearby except her physician who is, unfortunately, right in London. Here we are," he said, stopping the cart and hopping out like a man in his forties. He took a key from his pocket and offered it to Morgan.

"Thanks," she said. "Let's have a look."

The building was old, but well cared for. Tapestries hung on most of the walls but appeared clean. The water worked when she tried it, and there was a fire laid in the grate.

"Looks like you are expecting someone at any minute," Morgan said, as she continued to look around at the exquisite decorating.

"We always keep it like this, just in case. But as Deidre said, the security issue is real. We've only had a couple of people stay."

"You could use this as a writing retreat," Morgan said.

"*Or you could use it as a writing retreat. C.S. Lewis did a lot of writing on this property,*" Henry thought to her, "*I'm not certain it's really safe to talk in the cottage, but we can think.*"

"When did you know you could do this mind transfer thing?" Morgan asked.

"When I was about twelve. I never told anyone, though, except Deidre. I was afraid something terrible might happen."

Morgan looked at Henry, and it soon dawned on her that he had never told anyone about his own abilities in order to protect himself and the people who were important to him.

"My boss, and my bosses boss know about my hearing. They've been protective of the information that I know of. James knows, and a few relatives. Only James knows about the new development of mind reading."

"The people who know about your telepathic hearing condition don't need to know about the new developments. In my experience, when people who wield power learn things about people who are different, whether that makes them something to fear or not, they try to manipulate it to their advantage. I've seen it happen with spies, soldiers, academics. Nobody is safe unless they can keep the power secret."

"But this...this power of mine is something I have freely given them in order to help do my job better."

"I am only saying that you must be careful, Morgan. Exercise caution, and listen to your gut. Come up and see me on your days off and I can probably help you direct it better. You can get good at dropping in on people because most of them are unsuspecting, and then you can tap into anyone you want without them knowing. I'll also teach you how to ward yourself against being read by anyone else. It'll help keep you safe."

"Thank you, Henry."

Henry winked at Morgan. "Well, what do you think of it? Want to come out some weekend and grab some rest and relaxation? There are wonderful places to wander and get lost around here. The pubs are good too."

"I'd like that very much," Morgan nodded.

Chapter Eight

A few days later found Morgan standing at the window to her office, looking at the rain below. It was a gloomy London day, and the people on the street though used to the weather, complained about it.

"Bloody weather," Morgan could hear a woman saying. *"I can't wait to get to Majorca in a few weeks and get away from all this."*

"You'll be on your honeymoon, Jan. I don't think you'll notice the weather," her friend laughed as their umbrellas collided briefly.

That's what I need, Morgan thought to herself. A little holiday time to get away from all this talk of drugs and shootings and zombies. She picked up the phone to call Deidre, and booked the cottage for a weekend two weeks out.

"Oh, before I let you go," Deidre said, "Henry mentioned you'd like some of my special tea. It will ward off any germs or bugs you may encounter."

This is code for Henry's warding me against others who can read my mind, Morgan thought. "Yes, I'd love to get some when I see you. All these airplanes and recirculating air are hard on a person," she said.

"Henry's coming to London on Friday to visit with some of his old friends. If you can meet with him at their favorite place, you can pick it up in person."

"That sounds good. Just tell me when and where."

Deidre provided the details for a pub in the heart of London, not far from the War Rooms where Morgan's office was.

Morgan's problems continued as more *Joy19* infiltration manifested. Police forces around the globe were stretched to the max, but just as disturbing were the numbers of dead as hospitals and morgues overflowed. Morgan deployed all twelve teams she was responsible for, and they were fanning out to strategic positions around the world, including one team that continued to work with Skelter in their attempts to contain the spread in America, and a team in China.

"It's not easy getting teams into China, and their security seems to sometimes be two steps ahead of us these days," Chief Commander Steeves said to Director Mullins and Morgan. Steeves looked like Morgan felt – tired and resigned. She was in a meeting that included the ACTI brass, and the Deputy Prime Minister of England, Franklin Edwards.

"The council of the European Union has approached us. They are alarmed at the reports of this drug, though we have not confided in them your theory that the drug could be a form of biological warfare," said a man with a lined face and concern in his voice. He looked at the screen in the front of the room and fiddled with his tie as he watched the dots showing incidents of confirmed drug reactions and shootings around the world. As the Deputy Prime Minister, he didn't have time to mince words. "Frankly, we've been so busy with Brexit, and the impending resignation of our prime minister, we haven't been paying much attention to it ourselves."

"It's alright they don't know," Morgan said. "For now, our teams need some space to work on the origin of the problem and circumvent something bigger. We can leave it to different local agencies to deal with things in their own countries. One problem I am keenly aware of is the potential for someone to imagine that there is a problem in a refugee camp or prison and then kill the entire population there."

Steeves cleared his throat as if to underline what Morgan had said. "Deputy Prime Minister Edwards, we need your support, and we'd also like to call on MI6 for some help. I'm sure they've got far more operatives on the ground in China that we do."

"We don't have many operatives in China anymore, but I'll see what I can do. What makes you think this *Joy19* is coming from China?"

"When we review what's happened since New Year's Eve and where the drug could be originating from, we developed two theories around China and Russia. However, we're convinced that Russia is committed to manipulating America in political and financial ways, and probably wouldn't go this far. Plus, we have seen incidents of the drug there in the past few days. On the other hand, China has been very open in stating they have little to lose by damaging the relationship with the Americans. It doesn't sit right, given that the United States is by far their biggest trading partner, but the U.S. has made several moves in the past couple of years that really pissed off the Chinese government. Security issues with their cellular technology is only a part of it and we know the technical and digital pieces are a large part of the issue."

"So because of these digital and technical issues, you think that China has taken a stand in biological warfare with the United States? Why do we need to be involved at all?" Edwards' brow was furrowed.

"The drugs are here in Britain already, spreading rapidly, and we don't have a way to stop them. If we cannot put a stop to this distribution the devastation to human life will be far more significant that any other drug issue in the past, Sir." Morgan sat back and rubbed her temple, indulging in a long blink where all she could see were orange flames licking an overcast sky.

James added, "We also have no reports of *Joy19* incidents in China. Not a single one. We thought it could be because they were suppressing information, but the alternative is that they sent the drugs out of the country and there aren't any coming back in yet."

"The Chinese though? Really?" The deputy prime minister ran his fingers through his hair as he looked to the group for answers.

"You alright, Morgan?" Steeves asked.

"Yes, of course. Just had a long night last night and haven't had enough coffee yet today." She replied. "Would anyone else like coffee, or tea?" She reached over to the intercom and buzzed Natalie.

After the meeting, Natalie came in to survey the dishes and said to Morgan, "You are paying me way too much to fetch coffee or do dishes, you know that right?"

"Agreed," Morgan said. "But we haven't got anyone else doing it just yet. We will. Listen, I have a job for you but I think to do this properly you need to move into James' open area and use his equipment. That way both of you can work on this together."

Natalie stopped stacking cups on the tray. "Certainly. What are you hoping to find?"

"I think with your research skills combined with James' tech skills, you can find information about China that could take us weeks to get if we wade through proper channels."

"Okay, that sounds good."

Morgan smiled, but the stress of this job was written across her face. "Natalie, I have a feeling this could be a long project. If there's someone in the admin pool that can do the digitizing, fetch coffee, and whatever, let's get them on it. If I really need someone to bring me cookies, I'll just have to manage. Your skill set is magnificent, and I want to squeeze everything out of you I can."

"Just so you know, Morgan, I'm ready though I don't want to be a field agent. I'd rather do everything I can from here at the office."

"That's good Natalie, because that's the kind of help I want."

Early Thursday morning, Morgan had just arrived at her desk and was wading unhappily through a pile of email. She closed her laptop screen enthusiastically when Natalie and James showed up at her door.

"Good morning Morgan," Natalie said as she put a full mug of coffee down on Morgan's desk.

"Morning, Nat," Morgan said. "And to you, James. What's happening? You're not supposed to be bringing me coffee."

"We've been at our desks since 0400 and it seems like a good time for a break. Besides, we have news." Natalie plopped herself down at the small meeting table, her hands patting her lap like an excited schoolchild.

"The anticipation is killing me," Morgan said, blowing across the hot liquid to cool it a bit as she looked expectantly at the two of them.

"Do you want some scotch in that," James said, looking around for a bottle. He remained standing, and looked prepared to dive into Morgan's desk drawer to find a bottle if needed.

"James, it's not even seven in the morning. It's a bit early for scotch, even for me," Morgan said from under her eyebrows.

James ran his fingers through unruly hair, the result of coming to work after a shower and then in his nervous excitement, raking his mop with his fingers repeatedly since. He had bags and dark circles under his eyes, Morgan noticed, but he was clearly enjoying himself.

"Morgan, we're so excited," Natalie said. "The Chinese have had such tight control over the internet that we weren't sure what we'd find, but there are several dark web sites that rebels have developed to avoid government restrictions. We unlocked a goldmine this morning."

"Can you come into the lair and have a look?" James asked, his hands on his hips and eyebrows raised.

"The lair," Morgan repeated.

"Yes, it's what we've decided to call our working area. It's not really an office, more of a cleverly shielded open area in the middle of the building. A lair," Natalie said, laughing.

Morgan followed the two of them down the hallway. Soon the data was projected on a screen hanging above James' workspace.

Morgan looked at the conversation transcripts appearing on the screen. "Okay, this is good work you guys. One question...how will we sort out what's genuine traffic and what the Chinese are putting out to send us up the wrong pole?" she asked. She sipped her coffee as she watched the information scrolling in.

"Wrong pole?" Natalie said, confused.

"Yeah, you know, the Chinese are great at tactics and they may have things out there deliberately to throw us off the trail," Morgan said. "Like flying a flag up a pole, but they could purposely be sending us up a different pole than the one we need."

"But we're not circling those poles, Morgan." James offered her a tube of chocolate covered biscuits as he rolled past her in his chair, crossing the room to tap a few keys from a different keyboard. "In the past, we've searched for trigger words or actions that signalled a covert operation. It's always a problem because, as you say, a foreign government will try to send us up the wrong pole. This time, we're searching for drug users, social misfits, people who hate their jobs. These are much more of a low value target, and there is no government interference or screening taking place."

"You're actually finding things out already?"

"Yes, and the deputy prime minister was very quick to get us some help from MI6. They are translating the information just as fast as they can, plus we had a conversation with their main team in China and he's confirmed that what we're hearing is part of the drug trade. Check this out." He tapped several areas of his screen and Chinese characters appeared alongside translated comments. "Here you can see conversations between people in an area outside of Beijing. And this one, in a city that does mainly manufacturing. Both areas are known for having people who work menial jobs for small pay. Look at this conversation, where these three people are texting back and forth about what seems innocuous, a dog meetup. Except when we go to monitor their other texts on platforms like WhereItsAt, these people using the app don't have dogs."

"Look here," James continued. "They are meeting up at dry cleaners, of all places. Chinese tradition is that a lot of people in these cities don't have washing machines in their house and if they do, they are a small machine. They hang all their things to dry because dryers are a luxury most cannot afford. The washing machines aren't big enough to wash things like bedspreads, or a winter coat, so people have to take those things to a dry cleaner. The dry cleaners are located in busy parts of town, in between all the shops, market stalls, street vendors...and they give people a place to meet and carry on all kinds of transactions."

"So they're using the dry cleaners to obscure the fact they are trading drugs?" Morgan asked.

"Sort of," Natalie said. "And they have created a code around dry cleaning, clothing terms, and dogs that seems to describe drugs. We've got a team from MI6 on the ground nearby, and an ACTI team will be there in about four hours."

"Keep me posted hourly, please. Good work, you two," Morgan said. She stood back, leaning against a table on the edge of the lair, watching them work.

Morgan went to the morning management meeting, where Steeves, Mullins, and the new psychologist were deep in discussion about *Joy19*.

"Morning folks, sorry I seem to be a bit late," Morgan said, pulling her chair in.

"You're not actually late," Steeves said gently. "We got an early start, but it seems like you did too. We're getting Dr. Bendar all caught up."

"Nice to meet you Doctor," Morgan nodded at the trim woman in a dark navy suit with a grey sweater under her jacket.

"And you, Director Winfeld," she said. Her hair was thick and wavy with far more grey hair than Morgan expected of an ACTI shrink, and her face was... familiar looking.

"We know each other," they both said at the same time.

"Bendar. Maggie Bendar," Morgan said.

"I think you had a different name when I met you," Dr. Bendar said, as a frown creased her forehead.

"You've got a good memory. Nowadays I go by Morgan Winfeld," Morgan said.

"You guys know each other? What's the chances of that?" Steeves asked.

"Slim I would think. Dr. Bendar and I met back at Dalhousie University. You were a grad student if I recall," Morgan said, looking at the doctor.

"Yes, I was," Dr. Bendar said. "I was in Halifax and working on my doctorate while my husband was sailing with the Canadian navy. When I finished grad school, I started to work in human intelligence, which was way more fun than being a student." Her blue eyes caught the light, along with her dangling earrings.

"Human intelligence sounds interesting. How long are you assigned here?" Morgan asked. "I'd love to go for drinks sometime and swap stories about Nova Scotia."

"We're hoping Dr. Bendar is here for a couple of years. There have been too many changes to our team lately, and having some continuity would be helpful," Steeves said nodding at the doctor.

"I can give you a couple of years for sure," Dr. Bendar said smiling. "My husband is posted here, and within the next couple of years we will make some decisions about what we're going to do next."

Morgan looked at the woman. She had to be in her early to mid fifties, and her body was well toned under her suit.

"What's your experience like working with the drug trade?" Morgan asked sincerely.

"Pretty extensive. It's been a fascinating way to observe and interfere with organized crime, including the drug trade, extortion, and human trafficking. It's also the reason I sit this straight," she smiled tightly.

"Can you talk about it?" Morgan asked. She liked this psychologist far more than the others that had worked with ACTI previously.

"I had an injury and went flying off a motorbike during a mission. Still having some back issues. Nothing that interferes with my job so long as I keep working out, you know." She smiled, and waved off the injury from their conversation.

"So you're also a field agent?" Morgan asked.

"Yes, but under self-imposed restrictions not to do anything stupid for at least a few more months," Dr. Bendar smiled.

"Well, if you ever want to get tortured and recover to the utmost of your range, I know a great physiotherapist in Ireland," Morgan said. "I highly recommend her."

"I might just take you up on that," Dr. Bendar said. "It's not as easy to recover from things as it used to be."

Early Friday morning, Morgan arrived in her office just in time to hear the news she had been dreading. At an internment camp near the U.S. and Mexican border, there was a woman in late pregnancy who became very ill. With no doctor nearby and her worsening state, women in the cages near her were yelling for the guards and crying. Border guards shot and killed the pregnant woman and then in the ensuing chaos, they fired on the surrounding cages, mostly filled with women and children. The first border guard they interviewed said that it looked like a *Joy19* reaction they had been warned about, but as it turned out, there were no street drugs in the facility at all. It turned out the dead woman had severe pre-eclampsia.

Morgan stopped by the lair to see what James and Natalie had found.

"The drugs are definitely coming from China," James said before Morgan could say hello. "They were developed in a government lab and then issued to students heading back to the U.S. in time for the January term. It looks like all of them flew from Peking to New York, rather than sending some from Hong Kong to LAX in time for New Year's. We have now had incidents in Los Angeles, but we don't know exactly when the drugs arrived there."

"They were well paid, to the extent the Chinese government has put them all on full scholarships that will pay for foreign university registration, including room and board plus a 'token of appreciation for services to the government'," Natalie said.

"Can we find these students and track them down in the U.S.? How'd they get through border security with these drugs?" Morgan asked.

"We've got your friends at the FBI working on where the students went. As for how they got through security, the usual approach is to try and throw off border security by bringing prohibited items through the airport, like meat," James said. "Dr. Bendar is looking at how the drugs are getting through and helping us pinpoint exactly where."

Morgan's cell buzzed, and she put Skelter on speaker phone so that James and Natalie could listen in.

"Hey Morgan, how are things? I have Platt here with me," Skelter said.

"Thanks for calling Skelter. Hi Platt. I have James and Natalie here. What have you found out?"

Skelter read from his notes. "Two students landed at LAX on December 29. They didn't live together but both went to the same university. Both were found dead today, not from drugs, though. Their apartments were tossed but nothing obvious was missing except their laptops and phones. We're processing both scenes now, and so far we know they were executed with a shot to the back of the head. Possibly they were being used as mules and then murdered by Chinese operatives once they got here so there were no loose ends. Or, the hand-off of the drugs may have gone bad. Platt will update you on New York."

"Hey all, Platt here. For New York we have record of six students landing at LaGuardia, two of them flew on to other airports; one to Florida and the other to Minneapolis. We have recovered those two, and have teams out looking for the rest of them here in New York. And, there's something weird."

"Okay let us have it," Morgan said. "You know how we love weird."

"Well, so far it looks like some of these people are legit students. But at least three of them are too old, judging by their photos and their applications for school. My theory is that they are Chinese covert ops. Well trained, planted here as students and they appear to be serious academics according to the university records, but that's not the only reason they are here."

"Interesting. Keep me posted." Morgan asked. She disconnected, and looked at James and Natalie. "I think it's time we had another talk with Dr. Meriweather."

Jacinda Lee, also known as Dr. Meriweather, had been arrested under suspicion of being a spy from China. The psychologist had been very careful with her words since her arrest, and admitted to nothing. Morgan and her team had been so busy that she hadn't been fully questioned, and Morgan felt like she didn't have enough questions to ask, until now. ACTIs investigation, when they leveraged MI6 information research in China along with Meriweather's maiden name and passport history, was more helpful. Maggie invited Dr. Bendar to observe the interview from behind the mirrored glass in the small interrogation room.

"And so, we meet again," Morgan said, sitting across from Meriweather. "I hope you're being treated well here." They were in a meeting room next to the one single holding cell that was within the building. There was a bank of windows covered in a metal grid along one wall, which was a lot more window than the one in Meriweather's cell.

"It's fine," Meriweather said. She was squinting against the intensity of the light streaming in and warming Morgan's back.

"If you feel you aren't being treated fairly or you have not been provided with basic necessities, you are permitted to report that."

"It's fine," Meriweather repeated.

"Would you like some coffee? We may be here for a while," Morgan said.

"No, thank you." Meriweather said in a clipped tone.

"You know, before the incident in my office where you were going to stab me we were getting along quite well. I don't see why that has to change," Morgan said. She was being cruel, and she knew it, but she didn't care.

Meriweather looked at Morgan. Her brown eyes were cold. Her long blond hair, which was accustomed to being pinned up against her head with the now confiscated hairpin dagger, hung loose and tangled around her shoulders.

Morgan looked back. "You can have access to the showers afterward if you like. I will find a female guard."

"Fuck you," Meriweather said.

"Suit yourself. I'll start then. Everything that takes place in this room is being recorded. This is mainly for my protection since you are being detained as a terrorist and, while you do have a guarantee that we will treat you appropriately under the law, I have no assurances that you won't lie about what happens here and as such the recording is necessary."

No reply came from Meriweather, so Morgan kept going.

"You have not been formally charged, but sometime after our conversation here you can expect charges related to espionage, treason, and attempted murder to start with. Since your actions represent hostility toward the Queen, it will be the Crown who charges and prosecutes your case. You can expect the most serious of repercussions should you be convicted. Do you understand this?"

"You're telling me this, but I have not been charged yet?"

"Correct. Now, first off, I want to ask you some questions that will bring us to some agreed facts."

"Don't we both need a lawyer for this?"

"No, I certainly don't. If you would like one, as it was explained at the time of your arrest, you can ask for one. Are you asking for a lawyer?"

"No," Meriweather replied slowly. "I'm not sure it would be a good idea."

"Fine, then let the recording show that you have clearly declined a lawyer at this stage. Remember, you can ask for one later," Morgan said. She wanted this conversation to be clear in both its intent and to reflect her professional conduct.

"How long have you been working for the Chinese government?"
No answer.

"Did they pay for your university education?"
No answer.

"This doesn't work if you don't answer me, you know that right?"

"*Fuck you,*" Morgan heard Meriweather think.

Morgan continued. "Look, I have some important questions that need to be asked relative to the Chinese government and their plans to use covert operators such as yourself. I'm investigating you being here, as well as some international incidents that have occurred recently. Are you going to answer my questions?"

"Probably not," Meriweather said, "*Because no matter what, someone is going to sneak in here and kill me. It doesn't matter to me whether I answer your questions or not.*"

Morgan decided to come around and try a different tack. "Look, I know you are probably feeling alone. One of the first rules of spy school is that if you get caught on foreign soil, you are on our own. No one is coming to help you, and I wouldn't be surprised if you think your life is at stake. My job includes trying to protect you from harm. You have my word on it."

Meriweather kept her mouth shut, but her mind was racing. "*You can't stop them. They are everywhere. Connected to everyone. There are more of them spread throughout England and all over Europe and the United States. Just because we don't look obviously Chinese doesn't mean we aren't loyal to China.*"

"Have you been approached here by anyone who threatened to hurt you if you talk to me?"

"No."

"Do you understand that it's part of my job to keep you safe? That if you provide some answers to these questions that help me do my job, I am still committed to keeping you alive?"

"Yes, I understand, but I don't believe that anyone is as committed as my employer at making sure I don't say anything. The funny thing is, I don't know anything anyway."

"You don't?"

"No," she laughed nervously. "I just got my psychology license, remember?"

"So you are saying that as a recent grad, you weren't told anything that might help you in your job."

"Right."

"Okay, we'll follow that line of thought. When did you complete your training as a covert agent? It's pretty obvious you know how to handle yourself in a fight."

She didn't answer aloud, but Meriweather thought, "*Dammit. She's right. Of course I can handle myself. All that time in University and with evenings and school holidays spent training, I'm a force to be reckoned with.*"

Morgan kept going. "Who is your employer? Why are they interested in infiltrating ACTI?"

Meriweather didn't offer an answer.

"I'd like for you to stay in this room while I try to reach your embassy and get in touch with your handler," Morgan said. "Not that I expect much. I don't imagine they were ready for you to get caught so quickly."

"Good luck finding them."

"We can find anyone," Morgan said. "It's a small country."

Morgan stopped in to see Dr. Bendar after the interview. "What do you think Doc? Anything to add or that I could be asking her?"

"Not so far, and you seem intuitive in your questions, thorough, yet working her answers in and building on what you have. You also seem to have scared her a little. Do you think you can find her boss?"

"I'm not certain. We aren't totally sure who he is."

"Do you think he's here in England?"

"Somebody will be. I would think their upper echelon is in the U.S. since Britain is small potatoes right now, but it hardly matters. I'm hoping she will think about it and be just scared enough to give me something after she has sat here for another day or two."

Morgan left the interrogation feeling strong. Although the conversation hadn't lead to anything, Meriweather was thinking hard about things. Morgan would drop in on her later, after Chief Commander Steeves had finished some high level digging around.

"James, how are things," she asked, entering the lair. The blinds were partly drawn in places to keep the sun from streaming in and interfering with the screens. The place looked darker than usual, and Morgan had a fleeting thought that it only needed a dragon and a few gargoyles to complete the look.

"The FBI have picked up all the Chinese students and they are holding most of them in New York, with the two outliers headed that way under FBI escort," he said. "How'd things go with Meriweather?"

"She's not talking, but she's got a lot on her mind if you know what I mean," Morgan said. "I'm off to meet with Henry briefly. He's here in London for a gathering of his cronies or something. Do you want anything?"

"Honestly, I'm hoping to knock off here soon and go catch a movie. It's just after 1900 hours and there's mayhem and superheroes to watch on the big screen. Much more fun than real life." He looked at her and she noted some sadness around his eyes.

"James are you okay? Is this taking too much of a toll on you?"

"I'm alright," he said. "I knew what I was getting into when I signed up for this, and I wouldn't want to be anywhere else, Morgan. I wouldn't mind some fun, however, and maybe a bag of popcorn."

"You going with some friends, or all on your own?" Morgan asked, worried for her young cousin and wanting him to take some time for fun and nonsense.

"There are a few of us going from here, you should try it sometime," he said, smiling.

When Morgan arrived at the pub to meet with Henry, she was ten minutes early. She'd hoped to be early enough to sip at a scotch and take the edge off, but when she heard a roaring laugh from the back corner and knew that Henry had already arrived.

"Hallo, Morgan," Henry said, standing to greet her. He gestured to the group at the table, and said grandly, "Fellas, this is Morgan. Morgan, these are the fellas. I think we've got a plan in place that'll help you out."

"Morgan, when the ol' doc asks, we come running. Besides, who doesn't want to spend a few nights in London locked up in some posh hotel and running shenanigans?" The man addressing her had a thick northern accent, and shaggy brown hair that stuck up in different directions. He stood, and stuck out his hand. "My name's Oliver, nice to meetcha, and this here is Max, he's French so sometimes it takes him a second to translate but he's a good mate. That there is Simon, and this as you know, is Henry."

"It's wonderful to meet all of you. Surprising, in so many good ways!"

Henry leaned over and whispered in her ear, "These are all the fellas you need to do that public service announcement stuff and to maybe run some data for you. They've all worked on the big three social platforms in one respect or another, and that guy there," he said pointing at Simon, "was my partner on the development of the world wide web. Anyone you need to get to, anywhere in the world, these guys can reach them."

Morgan cleared her throat and looked at the men around the two small tables that had been pushed together. Henry pushed a chair behind her knees and she sat down heavily. "I'm kind of surprised to be honest, I mean, I put out a call for help, but I never expected all of you."

"Well, we've been sitting on our arses for months," Max said. "Arses is the right word here, no?" he laughed and his straight white teeth stood out against a black moustache and greying beard. His friends roared and the ones near him clapped his shoulders to congratulate his correct use of the word 'arse.'

"Have you all got somewhere to stay tonight?" Morgan asked.

"Yeah, we are at a fancy pants hotel down the street from here, and then in the morning we will gather together and get to work. Just tell us what you need."

"Let's meet at my office. You bring your gear, and we can leverage our security to make sure no one figures out what you are up to," she offered.

"We are simply bunch of grown up hackers, Morgan," Simon said, smiling. "We travel with our own means of security, but we will go wherever you need us to be."

"Our office is set up with great tech, and you won't run into restricted bandwidths or Peeping Toms on your network, I hope. I'll make sure my top two techs are there to brief you on where things have got so far. I can't tell you how happy I am you're here. What time shall we meet?"

"Not too early," Henry said. "These fellas tend to be night owls rather than morning people, isn't that right gentlemen?"

"Yes and no," laughed Max. "At my age I have to get up to the bathroom in the middle of the night, so I can either get dressed at five a.m. or nine. There is no in between."

"How about if we have brunch ready for you at nine thirty. Sound okay?" Morgan left the bar on cloud nine, texting Natalie as she walked back to the office and her little cot in the dorm room. Natalie's phone replied with an auto response.

Oh right, if James is at the movies with friends from work, it makes sense that Natalie is there too. Hopefully they are both up for coming in tomorrow so we can get things rolling. And, I had better find somewhere to order breakfast.

She called the same fancy hotel the fellas were staying at, and ordered a huge breakfast.

Saturday started bright and early for Morgan. She needed to arrange security for her guests, but had no idea what their last names were. She called Steeves at home and told him what she was up to, and then let him handle the arrangements. Next she called James, and planned to call Natalie, to see if they would mind donating yet another Saturday to the cause.

"Wait one," James said. "I can check with Natalie. She's right here."

Morgan bit her tongue.

"Yup," James said a moment later. "She'll be there too. Um, we might not come in together though, you know, just for optics."

"Uh James, you know the cat's out of the bag now that I know that you two are a thing, don't you?" Morgan laughed. "Besides that, you guys did a lousy job if you were trying to keep this a secret."

"There aren't any secrets with you Morgan, I know. But you also know how it is," James said softly.

"I sure do, James. We do dangerous work, and it's hard to find compatible people who don't object to the risk, schedules, and crazy." She rang off, suddenly wondering what Platt was up to. She'd hardly had a chance to think about him since returning from New York.

The Fellas, as Morgan started to call them, arrived together just after breakfast had arrived, and about ten minutes before they were expected. The room buzzed with their energy.

"You guys are like a bunch of kids in a candy store," Morgan said as she popped a hot greasy sausage into her mouth.

"Seriously, Morgan, I have dreamed about helping spies for my entire career. Now's my chance and I want to make the most of it," Max said. He smiled a big smile, and Morgan found herself thinking of Platt once again. *Focus Morgan, this is not the time for distractions.*

"First, I will need you all to sign a non-disclosure statement," Morgan said, swallowing thoughtfully, "and then as we get to work we will be running your security checks, because that makes it easier for me to let you go to the bathroom while you're here. So, if there's anything I should know before hand, tell me now."

Henry held up his hand as the group began to murmur. "Morgan you know that we don't call ourselves 'friendly hackers' for nothing. Most of us have been arrested at one time or another for protests or causing security breaches. And, though myself and Simon were the subject of a couple of arrest warrants early in the days of the web, the charges were dropped. Since then, we've been granted security clearances with the FBI, MI6, and all that."

"Not this agency though, I suspect," Morgan said. "And we've recently had a breach here, so I am trying to be cautious without creating delays. I can call my U.S. counterparts and start the ball rolling here."

"Let me know if I can assist," Henry said, then he jumped quickly out of his chair. "I nearly forgot to give you Deidre's tea. This will help you." He pulled a box of tea from his backpack, and offered it to her. There was no label on the box, just pictures of oranges and a bunch of herbs that Morgan didn't recognize.

"How does it work, exactly, Henry?" she asked.

Simon spoke up from across the table. "Henry thinks it is some kind of magic potion and it keeps you healthy when you fly or are around people with germs. I haven't had a cold or even a runny nose in ten years. Tastes like piss though, so make sure you put some honey in it."

Morgan decided to pop inside Simon's brain. *Hmm. Go figure. He really thinks it is a health tonic.* She didn't continue reading his mind long once his thoughts were flooded with computer programs, ones, and zeroes.

"I am sorry it doesn't taste the best. It shouldn't interfere with your functioning at all, and you only need to take it twice a week. Try some while I'm here, and then we can test it out." Henry rubbed his hands together, ready to get at his keyboard.

"How long does it last," Morgan asked softly, not sure she liked Simon's endorsement.

"Less time than a tattoo on your ribcage, which is the other option, about 100 hours."

Morgan tapped the button on the kettle and it quickly rumbled to life. Once the foul smelling bag was in the water she spooned some honey into the mug to take the edge off the flavor. As she returned to the lair to see how everyone was getting on, Simon was deep in conversation with Natalie and James.

"See here," he motioned at the screen. "You are right that's what we'd call dark web China. However, I think judging by the translations you've received, these are mostly hackers in here."

"What about the dry cleaners and their chat?" Natalie wanted to know.

"I think you're definitely getting close to them and you are in the right networks, but I'm looking for orders and I don't see them. We should see instructions, drop offs and pick ups done on burner phones, quickly created social accounts, that kind of thing, but China could be different. Let's see what's happening in Taiwan. Since Taiwan considers itself an independent state, but China considers it as part of China, there is always interesting stuff to eavesdrop on," Simon said. James watched Simon work through screens and code.

"See here," Simon said, "this is a bump in police calls in Taipei. And this is a report of hospital closures. When you visit Taiwan, it's a hodgepodge of languages, but predominantly Mandarin for residents nowadays, though for visitors and business dealings, they speak English."

"You speak Mandarin," Natalie said, in awe of this man whose computer skills were challenging her to learn more.

"Yeah, and a few other languages. They are as much a fascination to me as code for a computer. Plus, it makes people laugh at me when I'm travelling because apparently my accents are terrible, and that's always fun...here," he said, "James and Natalie see this? It's an exception...the orders aren't originating inside of China..."

Morgan left them and stopped to see what Henry and Max were up to. "Morgan your Public Service Announcements will be ready to go soon. We need to decide which particular languages you want them in."

"As many of the major languages as you can manage, with back up in English."

"We are designing a series of landing pages with access to lots of information for people to read. They will think they are seeing information from drug enforcement agencies, health care, and government. We should include some animated video too –

something that engages the audience but offers the same message. It'll cost a few bucks, but you will likely get better penetration with your message."

"How much money are we talking?" Morgan asked.

"About $50 will get it animated, translated in a dozen languages...more if you want." Henry said.

"How is it we didn't know these things? $50 and we could be saving all these lives?" Morgan was stunned.

"Remember that the average person, or corporation, doesn't have access to us. We don't normally give this stuff away. Morgan, try not to get too wrapped up in the human nature that it takes to wreak this kind of devastation on others. It'll eat you up inside. Just leave us to it, and we'll tell the bots what to do," Henry said. "Two hours or so and this will all be ready to go."

"Globally?" Morgan said.

"We can send it to Mars if you want," he smiled.

Chapter Nine

"Hey Skelter, how're the wife and kids doing?" Morgan's question was quick and without preamble.

"You have no idea how awful that sounds, do you Morgan?" Skelter asked, pretending to be stern.

"Of course I do," she said contritely, then sighed. "Well, can I at least get full marks for trying to remember the small talk?"

"Yes, absolutely. You get gold stars for this call," Skelter laughed. Morgan felt better just hearing the laughter. Now that this day was coming under some degree of control, she felt better all over.

"I just wanted to let you know that the Public Service Announcements are out, and have been flooding the web and all kinds of places I didn't know existed yesterday."

"How the hell did you get them to agree to help? For that matter, who helped?" Skelter asked.

"Remember those founders of the big social media and web platforms I wanted to invite to work with us, but I couldn't get them to call me back? Well, the team here got hold of someone who is both well connected and has smart friends."

"What'd you have to do to get their help? Sell your soul?" Skelter's voice was serious now.

"Nope, they were happy to be asked. Honoured actually right up until they were briefed on what was happening and then they were also pissed off at what humans will do to kill one another. Oh, and I fed them. A lot. The food bill is going to be out of this world but worth it."

"Alright, so what's the next step?"

"Can you come over here for a meeting? I know it's a long way and the alternative is that I could come there but I'd like you to see what's going on here. And bring Platt if you can."

"Not sure how I can expense Platt exactly. He's a New York City cop if you recall."

"Yeah, but he is assigned to you and me as part of this mission."

"I'll see what I can do."

"If you get any flack, tell Director Bilous that Platt is part of this team and a former Marine. I can call too if you need me too."

Skelter laughed again. "I think I have it covered. Don't worry. We will see you Monday."

When Morgan got off the phone with Skelter, she texted Platt.

I hear you are coming to London. Please
bring a jar of instant espresso
as I am unable to find it here.

After a pause that was just about long enough for Skelter to have filled Platt in on the travel plan, the return message was brief. It's not that Morgan had looked for the espresso in London, but if she had the time she was pretty sure she wouldn't have found it.

Roger. On it.

When he arrived Monday afternoon with Skelter, Platt was hesitant. He held out an open jar of espresso and handed it to Morgan. "With my apologies, I had to steal this from the break room at the station. There wasn't time to pick up any shopping," he said.

"It's okay," Morgan said. "It was really a ruse just to make sure you were coming."

"Wouldn't miss it for the world," he said. He moved closer to Morgan out of hearing range to the others as they gathered in the lair. "It's really good to see you."

"You too," Morgan smiled. "You have no idea." She moved to a central spot in the room and did some quick introductions followed by a brief on the next steps they would take together. She introduced The Fellas, Steckler, Platt, James, and Natalie as integral people who had created an avenue to build the Public Service Announcements, PSAs, and introduced Chief Commander Steeves, and Director Mullins. "I'm so glad to have you all here. Now that the PSAs have been issued I feel like we can shift into the next phase of this operation and I appreciate you being here as we discuss the next steps. My objectives include putting a stop to this infiltration of *Joy19* without an act of war. That's going to require input from everyone in this room as well as some of our field agents. Once we have some options, we'll prepare a brief that Chief Commander Steeves will share with some select world leaders."

Steeves added, "So far, we're working with senior staff in Britain, Canada, America, and Russia. That's a small but very powerful representation of where this drug has shown up."

"Having *Joy19* show up in Moscow as violently as it did, the Russians didn't hesitate at accepting the invitation," Steeves said, with his hands shoved uncharacteristically in his pockets.

Morgan said, "We also need to see what's happening in India. As a close neighbour to China but not allied with them they will be important. I understand they don't want to be seen setting alliances with Britain since they are still perceived as a colonizer there, but India has a huge military and plenty of history with China...do we have *Joy19* reports from India, James?"

James shook his head no, and simultaneously began tapping on a screen looking for information.

"How is this not an act of war on China's part?" Natalie asked. "I'm not as current on politics, maybe, but the planned murder of innocent citizens whether it's from a drug or a bomb seems like an act of war to me."

Chief Commander Steeves cleared his throat and spoke with authority. "It is most certainly an act of war, Miss Wooden. But, we don't, any of us, want to be 'at' war with China. While it appears they are at some level responsible for the creation and distribution of *Joy19* and their actions are deplorable, we know that to start a full scale war with them would begin something out of a nightmare. Their desire to be the biggest most powerful economy in the world is no secret, nor is their desire to meet their needs by killing anyone who opposes them. Full out battle with them could be something none of us ever fully recover from."

"None of us want an all out war," Morgan said. She was standing in front of the group, her hands clasped in front of her. "The global economy we live in now means that each country is in complicated financial relationships with each other. The Chinese have invested billions of dollars in American, British, Russian, and Canadian real estate and businesses but it's not one sided. Joint ventures, shared research, trade agreements all mean that we are as equally connected to them as they are to us. Going to war doesn't make sense for any of us, because it could depress all of our economies significantly. We've also got to consider that we recently detained someone who is a Chinese operative. How many other operatives are out and about from any one of our countries? The deeper we dig into this, and – no matter what evidence we are currently looking at – we also have to consider if someone else is involved, alongside or backing China."

Skelter scowled, and stood up ready to pounce on an invisible target. "What do you mean, Winfeld? All the evidence you've gathered points to China at the heart of *Joy19*."

"I've been reviewing the politics of all this, as well as some of the data that James, Natalie, and The Fellas have kindly gathered for us. Look at how many incidents in the past three years have occurred, specifically in the U.S., that we initially thought was an act of terrorism, but then we discovered they were domestic issues. They ended up being caused by Americans, acting alone or within a very tiny, select group of people. Individuals with a huge chip on their shoulder, out to wreak maximum damage."

"Seriously Winfeld? You think this could be domestic?" The lines in Skelter's face were askew as he went from frowning to perplexed to rage.

"I'm just saying that before we declare war on China, we need to step back and consider the evidence," Morgan said quietly. "I'm not saying I like what I am thinking, I'm just saying that it's a theory we need to consider. Henry, can you present what you've got, please."

Skelter sat, looked around the room, and said, "Sometimes I hate this job, knowing the things that ordinary people should never know."

Natalie looked up from her tablet where she had been recording notes. "So," she said tucking her hair behind her ear, "you're saying that someone is making it look like the Chinese are doing this, meaning they've got some sophisticated skills, but it's not the Chinese."

Henry stepped into a quiet moment, and with his hands held in front of him, he looked at the group. "It's not certain, but it seems possible that there could be someone framing China for what's happening, or paying for all of this to throw blame on China. It's also possible that the Chinese are issuing information in the hopes of throwing us off. The intel we have isn't clear yet. It's also remotely possible that the Chinese are on to us and are throwing out diversions so we get off their ass."

"I thought the Chinese weren't going to be able to detect the snooping we were doing," Morgan said.

"Well, something is happening somewhere," Henry said.

"What should I be telling the leaders we have gathering for this call?" Steeves asked. "I was ready to go in there and tell them to clean their guns. Now it sounds like we need to put the brakes on." The group began to murmur.

Henry held up his hand, "Gentlefolk, let me share some data with you. Here you can see what we've done...with the work that James and Natalie started, we've increased the scope of their algorithm, and then created some additional ones. We are getting information on China and the U.S., including monitoring drug trafficking. We have discovered drugs being manufactured and funneled from a couple of locations in China, warehouses or manufacturing plants, and we don't know if it's your *Joy19* yet but it's likely. We're also looking at the dry cleaners who seem to be handling the distribution, particularly to university students who are registered at American universities, but that will take some time to flesh out."

"You're learning all this from...a bunch of data?" Platt asked, impressed.

"Yes, and there's more. Drug money is never an easy thing to follow, but when it's big money and there is money laundering going on, it can be done. Max here set out looking for deposits, withdrawals, and cryptocurrency exchanges. He's also looking for an uptick in prepaid credit card usage. We should be able to get more information to you in three or four days."

Steeves look at the group before he spoke, his voice dark and deep. "The drugs have made it into Canada, of course, and the Canadian Prime Minister is going to be on this upcoming call with me, but they do a lot of trade with China just like everyone does. They are, I assume, going to tread very cautiously here. They pissed off the Chinese government last year when they held a Chinese executive from a big tech company. The U.S. wanted to extradite her to face charges, Canada picked her up, and in retaliation for that, the Chinese arrested a couple of Canadian businessmen. They both face life in prison if the Chinese have their way. The relationship between Canada and China right now is not positive."

"What about a response from Britain?" Morgan asked.

"The British have a sizeable military, but nowhere near the size of China, India, or the U.S. And, Britain has been so distracted with Brexit they've hardly looked at this. I think they'll need international help to protect themselves from China before they can offer much value in a state of conflict," Steeves said.

"With Brexit delayed again but looking imminent for October, it's not a given that they'll be getting much support from the EU," James said quietly, rubbing his stubbled chin. "Holy shit, this is getting way bigger than I thought it was going to get, and I knew it was getting big."

Steckler looked around the room. "The Americans are not unprepared for something like this."

"I think that it's almost time this issue was handed off to government leaders, but we need more data, as you are suggesting," Steeves said.

"So what's our next step?" Morgan asked, her eyes brooding and the stab of a headache starting at the back of her neck.

Steeves let out a rumbling sigh. "Well, first we are meeting at my place for our Christmas in January party at 2000 hours. You are all expected, including Henry and The Fellas, agent Skelter, and Sergeant Platt. We'll let the data continue to grow tomorrow and into Monday before we meet again."

Platt looked over at Morgan, "A Christmas party? What's that all about?"

"Steeves is big on the holidays, and he waited until I got back to hold the work party. We don't have to go for long, but it's good to go."

"So we have to go?" Platt asked.

"Yep," Morgan said. "And we'd better leave now to get things ready or else we'll be late."

"Where are we going exactly," Skelter asked. "I had no idea there was a function this weekend."

"It's not that far from here. We can take a cab and still have you back at your hotel before midnight," Morgan said. She had mixed feelings about the party. They had far too much work to do, but she knew that Steeves had delayed his customary gathering on her behalf. She caught herself rubbing the back of her neck and wondered what it was that had her spidey senses reacting.

Steeves came around the corner and answered the unspoken questions. "I know you've got tons to do and want to get at it. But having an engagement will fill a few hours while we wait for more data and for the world leaders to get their plans in shape. Besides, you all need a break, some food, drinks, and maybe a few laughs. I promise it'll be more fun than waiting for your computer to ping."

Morgan smiled. "I know it will be too. We'll be there with bells on."

"Right. Good," Steeves said.

Morgan, together with Platt and Skelter, hailed a cab for the 25 minute ride north to Steeves' home. They were quiet as they rode along. James and Natalie would follow in another cab, along with other members of ACTI, plus The Fellas.

As the taxi jostled along busy, crowded streets Morgan felt the ping of a text arriving to her phone but she didn't dig it out of her pocket. *It's almost impossible to move inside this taxi, no need to jab anyone with my elbow. Except Platt maybe...I could jab him.* She stared out the window, but there wasn't much to see in the early darkness, aside from headlights and streetlamps, and people wrapped in their long scarves and warm coats.

Her phone buzzed again and Skelter looked at her. "You going to get that?" he said. "I can't believe you can receive a text and not answer it straightaway."

"I thought I'd wait until we arrived so I'm not elbowing you guys," Morgan said. Her phone buzzed again and she sighed, exasperated, then leaned over against Platt as she fished it from the inside pocket of her leather coat.

There were several messages from James:

Emerg at destination.

Cancel taxi.

Emerg at guvnor's house. Abort.

Emerg at destination. Abort visit.

"What the hell?" Morgan said. She showed the messages to Skelter and Platt so as not to alert their driver, and tapped out the shortcut to call James.

"Jesus, you weren't answering. Are you okay?" James sounded out of breath.

"Of course, I'm okay. What the hell is going on, and remember this is not a secure line," she said. "You're supposed to be right behind me, remember?"

"There has been an incident at your destination. I don't have any details, but you need to change plans immediately," he said. His voice was strained, but his message was clear.

"We're only five minutes from our destination now. Will assess and then call you."

"Be careful Morgan. Henry is here with me and he says be very careful."

The traffic was blocked at the end of Steeves' street, and the cab came to a halt. Morgan handed the driver cash as Skelter and Platt exited the car, and then she did the same.

"What do you think it is?" Skelter asked looking around. He patted under his arm where his sidearm normally sat in its holster. The look on his face registering that he was unarmed and on foreign soil could not have been missed by anyone.

"Not sure," Morgan said, looking around the street. The streetlights were on and a few porchlights.

"It looks pretty bright further up the street," Platt said. "Let's cross the street and take it slowly."

People were gathering on the pavement, and it wasn't long before the trio knew there had been some kind of an explosion up the street. They proceeded quickly, Morgan grateful she was able to carry her gun in England, though she left it tucked in the holster since there were members of the public around. Soon they could see flames licking at the eaves of a three story townhouse, connected on either side to a row of houses that spanned the length of the street.

"What's the chances of that being Steeves' house," Skelter exclaimed.

"You mean what's left of Steeves' house," Morgan said. "That's either his place or his immediate neighbour. I can't tell just yet."

They reached the smoking hull as Steeves exited the front door half dragging and half carrying someone in a chef's coat. Both men were singed by the blast, and Steeves pointed over his shoulder, "There's no one else inside, they all got out the back, but I'm not sure about the neighbors."

Platt sprang to the closest neighbor and Skelter moved off to the house on the other side. Morgan eased the cook onto the ground with Steeves, and then looked closely at her boss. "Are you hurt?" At the same time, she was dialing 999 on her phone, the emergency number used throughout the United Kingdom.

"I'm fine. That was no household accident Winfeld. Someone tossed explosives through the back and front of the house at the same time, and then buggered off."

"Did you see anything?"

"Not a damned thing. It was dark out and I couldn't do much more than try to get my breath and then get out," he said as he ran his fingers through his thick grey hair, the lines around his eyes looking exaggerated because of the smoke.

Morgan spoke with the emergency operator quickly, and though they wanted to keep her on the line she disconnected once she gave them the initial details, and then she placed a call to James.

"James, this was a bombing. Some minor injuries, Steeves is alright."

"Be careful," James said. "Henry couldn't emphasize enough what danger you are all in."

"I know, my hair's standing up on the back of my neck as it is," she said.

Platt ran back to her, and said that no one seemed home at the neighboring house. Morgan looked at the cook on the ground, who was coughing but trying to sit up.

"Did you see anything?" Morgan asked as she knelt beside him. Her voice was calm. "Just lie down, the ambulance will be here shortly."

"Saw nothin' except some kind of canister come right through the window into the kitchen and another through the door to the garden." He gasped and coughed. Morgan saw the red dot of a laser stand out starkly on his blackened chef's coat. "Take cover!" she yelled.

Shots quickly followed, with one just missing the cook as Morgan rolled him onto his side and out of the way of the laser. He quickly got himself on all fours and looked around before collapsing on the ground. Steeves pulled out his revolver and Morgan drew hers, seeking the direction of the shooter.

"Up there," Platt said nodding but knowing not to point using his finger. "There's a red glow up in the window of the place to our right. Must be a shooter."

The group of them moved quickly around parked vehicles, placing the catering van between them and the shooter. Skelter joined them, dodging a shot from the window.

"This is not a safe place if that bloke hits a petrol tank," Steeves said in a stage whisper.

"Well, what do you recommend?" Morgan snapped at him. "We're kinda stuck for good options here."

"I'll cover you," he said. "We're the only two with weapons. You move down a couple of car lengths and see if you can get a better shot."

"Roger that," Morgan said. She crouched low and passed the first car, but the shooter must've seen her moving because there was a shot that brushed the air near her head as she moved to the next car. *That was closer than I like,* she thought, crouching as low as she could possibly squeeze herself.

She moved quickly around the end of the next vehicle, taking advantage of the shadows and raising herself up slightly to look at the window. She couldn't see anything to shoot but felt a sensation behind her, and turned slightly as someone came up on her left side with a knife drawn. She used the gun in her hand to strike out at the knife, knocking the blade briefly and just enough to interrupt the assailant. Morgan fired her weapon and heard a grunt and thud as the bullet found its target. Immediately, there was a stream of bullets from an automatic weapon assailing her from the window. She laid flat on the ground again, feeling damp pavement soak through her sweater and bra. *Well that pissed him off. Fuck, it's cold here ... now wait Winfeld, until he needs to reload.* She heard the shooting pause, scrambled up, and moved back to where Steeves was. He'd been shot in his upper right arm, and was gasping as he leaned against the car. Platt took Steeves' weapon and trained it on the window.

"He's had enough time to move rooms in addition to reloading," Platt said. His voice was steady, and the years of combat and police training showed in his calm stance and demeanor.

Skelter saw to Steeves. "He's not bleeding too bad, but we need that ambulance," Skelter said. The pitch of his voice was a little higher than normal, but Morgan could see he was managing fine. He pulled off his jacket and removed his shirt, pulling at it to tear a crude strip off for wrapping around Steeves' arm.

"The ambulance will stay at the end of the street. They'll come closer once the shooting stops." Morgan looked around. The row houses were all connected, making it impossible to sneak through to the back without going through Steeves' smouldering home. "I really don't like how this guy has us pinned down. If he has anymore of those bombs, we're sitting ducks," she said. She looked over at the cook. His face was sweating, and his eyes barely open. He was going into shock.

"Hey buddy," she said to him. "Stay with us now. You're dealing with some smoke, and we'll get you some oxygen and water just as soon as we can. Are you okay otherwise?"

He mumbled, and Morgan put her hand on his leg. She could feel the muscles shaking as he started to lose control. "Buddy, what's your name? C'mon, don't pass out on me. What's your name?"

"N...Neil," he croaked softly. "Name's Neil. I'm j...just a cook."

"Did your chef get out of the kitchen okay Neil? Did he go out the back?"

"Y...yeah. I was closer to the front of the kitchen, and got knocked down in the blast. That guy there," he said pointing to Steeves, "pulled me out the front door."

"Do you have your boss's number in your phone? Can I call him?" Morgan asked gently. Platt was looking at her with a 'what the fuck' expression on his face as Neil dug the phone out from the front pocket of his smock and handed it to her shakily.

The phone was answered quickly. "Neil, Neil, you alright?"

"Neil's okay, we got him out the front of the building, but he's swallowed some smoke. My name is Morgan, and we are kinda pinned down out here. What's your name? Can you tell me where you are?"

"My name is Walter," he pronounced it somewhere between Walter and Valter, in heavily accented English. "Walter Snow. We are in the lane a few doors over, but still close. There's three of us. No one is hurt."

"Walter, I want you to get out of the way."

"Sure, sure, tell me what to do." Morgan could hear him dragging on a cigarette.

"Walter, put that cigarette out so no one can see where you are, first of all. There is a bad guy in the house next door, and we also were attacked by someone on the street out front. You need to be really careful, okay?"

"Ya, ya, okay. Cigarette is out. You guys, you guys, put those smokes out," she could hear him telling the others.

"Good. Down at the end of our street is an ambulance, and there will be police shortly. I want the police to come down here, very carefully, with armour on, and help us get two injured men out of here. Tell them there is at least one active shooter."

"Oh my god...okay, we are moving that way now. We will get police for you." *He either has military training or he was a cop.* She leaned in to listen as Walter gave orders to the caterers. "Stay low, eyes everywhere in case there is someone out here," Walter said.

Morgan called 999 again and spoke with the operator. "I am on a regular cell phone. Please note the emergency code is 98742 and I have an injured big bird here. There is hostile activity at this site. Requesting armoured response to remove the injured, and then implement code four niner seven," she said.

"Roger," said the operator. "Let me put you through to the site commander. They are nearly on site."

Morgan handed the phone to Steeves as the curtain moved at the upstairs window.

"Platt, I have six shots left in this clip and no more ammo after that. How many shots have you fired?"

"Five," Platt said.

"When I went up to knock on that door and check everyone had evacuated there was no response but by now the guy may have boobie trapped the front door," Platt said quietly.

"The back wall of all these places is glass windows along the whole expanse of the main floor," Steeves said, closing his eyes briefly. Morgan could see him fighting back nausea as he tried to stave off the shock that was threatening. "If you can smoke bomb the back, you might drive him out. Better though if you could also smoke bomb the upstairs where he is hanging out." He was speaking to the site commander by phone, just loud enough so that Morgan could hear.

Skelter spoke from the dark shadows. "I see movement at the main floor window. Not sure if that's our original shooter or a backup."

"Fuck," Morgan said. "This is about to get messy." She shifted her feet, which were threatening to go numb as she maintained a low squat. Tilting her head forward, she leaned in to listen. It only took a few seconds before she could hear people speaking abruptly, using short, clipped remarks. Two voices at first, then a third. *Some kind of Asian language, probably Cantonese, but fuck knows what they are talking about.*

"Skelter, can you check the guy that had the knife, have a look at his face and tell us if he is Asian. Look for ID. Not that I would expect ID, but you never know." Morgan said.

"One sec," he replied, doing his best to duck walk over to the dead figure spread eagle on the road. He pulled the black fabric mask off the dead man's face. "Asian, mid- thirties," he said.

Steeves opened his eyes, and said quietly to Morgan. "You're on to something. What is it?"

"I can hear Cantonese, I think, two but maybe three voices. These guys will be armed up to the teeth in there, but I can't understand what they are waiting for."

Steeves sighed. "I had a couple of high profile guests coming here tonight, not just your friend Henry, but also two members of the royal family. Nobody knows about the guestlist, unless someone coming here let something slip. Then again I wouldn't be surprised if that arsepick I met for lunch about Meriweather decided to follow me around."

"Arsepick?" Morgan had to suppress a giggle. "What is an arsepick exactly?"

"Exactly what it sounds like," Steeves said with a grimace. "He's not a nice man, way up in the Chinese government in covert ops even though he pretends to be an ambassador, and not to be trusted. These guys could be waiting on orders from him."

"Do you think he is directing this?" Morgan asked in a stage whisper.

"Certainly within the realm of what's possible," Steeves said.

Morgan sighed loudly. "Steeves, Platt and I have about twelve bullets between us, and I expect these guys have an arsenal. A couple of small rocket launchers however, and we could take out the entire house, though the houses on either side – including yours – could suffer plenty of collateral damage."

"Well, that will have me staying in a room at the War Rooms possibly right next to you for a while, so as long as you don't mind a little extra company, go ahead and blow it all up."

"Maybe I'll check and see if they have smoke cannisters before we go ruining everything here," she said. She took the phone from Steeves' shaking hands and spoke with the site commander. He was planning to sneak eight men to her location, one of whom was a medic. All were in tactical gear. She briefed him on the situation and asked him to bring the right weaponry. He grunted his agreement as he signed off the phone.

It took another forty-five minutes for streetlights and power to get cut off along the street. The police were busy evacuating people as quietly as possible from surrounding properties. Another fifteen minutes elapsed as the tactical squad made their way down the street.

By then, Steeves had lost a lot of blood despite having Skelter's bright white dress shirt tied around his upper arm, though Steeves was still working his phone and in touch with James as they tried to locate the Chinese Ambassador. Neil was unconscious, his breath coming in rough gasps as his throat and lungs screamed for air.

The tactical team leader arrived with an arsenal, and Morgan shared her suspicions that the men hiding inside the house were outfitted in night vision goggles and probably knew exactly what was going on along the street. Team leader Andrews nodded his understanding, and agreed that they should wait to move the injured until after their initial foray against the house. He used hand signals to ensure his men had their sites set on three access points at the front of the house. A second team was focussed on the rear of the old row house, beautifully preserved for generations and about to undergo an unrequested remodeling.

The medic opened blast blankets and wrapped them Steeves and Neil to protect them from fallout.

"I think he wants some water," Morgan said, looking at the young man. His lips had swollen in the time they had been waiting, and his breathing was ragged.

"No water yet," said the medic. "Oxygen first 'til we can tell how much fire or smoke he took in. I'll start an intravenous as soon as we get him to the ambulance." He covered Neil's mouth and nose with a portable oxygen mask.

As the tactical team readied themselves and took aim on the house, Morgan and Platt did the same with their revolvers. Platt fished out a small gun from his holster on his prosthesis and Morgan looked at him with admiration. He handed the pistol to Skelter.

"That thing legal for you to have here?" Morgan whispered.

"Nope," he said, grinning at her, "and its only a twenty-two so the bullets won't go far but it can't hurt."

"Nicely done, Platt," Skelter said. He looked over at Platt and winked.

Their eyes had adjusted to the pitch black of a cloudy January night. When one of the curtains moved in the house and released a shard of light, they took aim. Andrews issued an order over the comms as his team simultaneously launched smoke cannisters. They fired random shots in the windows. Morgan could hear a man moaning inside the house. One shooter jumped from the top window to avoid the smoke, the unmistakable sound of bones breaking as he landed feet first and collapsed. A second man came through the front door with his hands in the air, tears and snot streaming down his face as he stumbled his way down the front steps. The tactical officers prepared to move in.

"Wait," Morgan yelled, "There could be one more inside."

"How do you know that?" Andrews called to her.

"Call it intuition," she said.

"No one has come out the back," Andrews relayed the information from his comms unit. "We will clear the house. You lot," he said pointing to Morgan, Skelter, and Platt, "stay here. I'll update you as soon as I can."

The tactical team entered the house from the front and back at the same time, stopping just long enough to handcuff the man by the front door. They entered carefully in case of a booby trap, but it had been disengaged when the second operative had made his exit. The third operative was dead inside the house. It looked like he had tripped over a small footstool and then banged his head on a solid corner of a wooden sideboard. Although the guy was wearing night vision goggles and they should have helped him see through the smoke, Andrews shrugged at one of his teammates, "Probably never figure that one out," he said drily.

The homeowners were found unhurt, despite spending several hours tied up, gagged, and locked in their ensuite bathroom. They were partially sheltered from the tear gas and hardly affected by it.

"Well done, Andrews. Thanks for coming and saving our asses," Morgan said, introducing him to the rest of the team.

"What were you lot doing here tonight?" Andrews asked.

"It was a belated Christmas party," Platt said, looking around at the mess from the explosions and the firefight. Among the debris was broken glass and shattered brick, two bodies, and fluttering police tape.

Morgan looked at Platt and took his hand, then reached over to Skelter, shirtless and starting to shiver under his jacket. "What do you say we head to the hospital to check on Steeves, and then go out for a drink?"

"Good idea," both men said together.

Chapter Ten

Morgan stretched in Platt's hotel bed. She looked over at him, still asleep, facing her while he slept on his side. There was no way for her to entertain him in her teeny room at the War Rooms, and she luxuriated for a moment in the large bed with soft sheets, right up to the point where she stretched just a little bit too far and got a sharp cramp in her calf. She quickly slipped from the bed and hobbled toward the bathroom to stretch the errant muscle. *God damn it that hurts. Must be from all that time squatting last night. Was that only last night? Fuck, talk about the worst Christmas party ever.* She put her hands on the sink and leaned forward with her heels on the floor, stretching her calf, and then did a couple of lunges.

"You okay?" Rob was sitting up in bed when she came out of the bathroom.

"Yeah, had a cramp. How are you? Your leg has got to feel like hell this morning."

"Stump's a little sore. I usually do more prep work for it before an op, but it's okay. Wanna grab a bite before you head to the office?"

"How'd you know I was going to head to the office?" She sat on the bed pulling on her socks and sweater.

"Because you said that's what you were doing this morning, and it's after 0800, so you probably feel like you're running late," he said, swinging himself to the edge of the bed and pulling a sock over his stump.

"You know me too well. Want to grab a bite on the way there?"

"I'd rather grab another bite right here right now," he said, mischief written across his face.

"Forget it cowboy. Nobody wants the hungover Morgan, least of all people she actually likes."

"Wait a minute...you like me? Really like me?" he smiled, and reached over to kiss her.

"What? Are you twelve year's old Rob?" she laughed. "I like you a lot, except when you wake up after a night cap that includes honey garlic wings and dark beer."

He grinned. "It's okay Morgan, I like you too. Now, are you too hungover for breakfast?"

"First of all, it's not possible for me to be too hungover for breakfast. Coffee and a breakfast muffin should fix everything, though some eggs benedict with bacon on the muffin wouldn't hurt, either."

"On a muffin?" he asked with his nose wrinkled.

"You'd call it an English muffin in the States, but here it's just a muffin or a breakfast muffin, and very different from the cupcake style thing you'd call a muffin back home."

"I have so much to learn," he said as he pulled his prosthesis over a clearly irritated looking stump. "Are you missing those New York pastrami sandwiches?"

"Yes and no. I'm pretty sure I gained ten pounds while I was there, and then there was that whole zombie thing going on to dampen my enthusiasm."

"There's a new vegan place that's opened around the corner from my building. They've got some pretty good stuff on the menu. Six kinds of sprouts and all that, and I haven't seen any zombies there yet. I think zombies prefer pizza."

"I'd have to stop at a hot dog cart and add some meat to anything that is labelled vegan, just so you know," she said, slipping her sweater over her head and noticing blood splatter on the sleeve.

"Goddamn it," she said, "I really liked this sweater. I think Steeves bled on me."

"Or it's from the guy you shot. He was pretty close." Rob looked closely at her sleeve.

"He was wasn't he? Dammit."

"Try not to dwell on it. It's only a small splatter and no one except you will even notice," he said, kissing her on the cheek.

"Yeah, sure Rob, but maybe you could loan me a t-shirt. We can eat and try to forget about the bad guy in the dark, fucking up our quest for world peace, plus the beggars ruined Christmas!"

"Beggars?"

"Yes, it's a term they use here. I don't like it quite as much as arsepick, but I like to keep my options open when it comes to cussing. You know Rob," she pulled the door shut behind them and they headed toward the elevator.

"What?" he replied, leaning over to kiss her on her cheek as they walked.

"I think we need to take a couple of days off and go to Oxford for some R and R. What do you think?"

"I think that sounds like a great idea. Let me talk with Skelter."

Skelter stepped out of his room and pulled the door closed loudly, then quickly moved toward them in order to catch the same elevator.

"Talk with Skelter about what?" he asked. "Wait, are you guys talking about me? What the hell!"

"That's a terrible imitation of me, Skelter," Morgan said. They laughed the laughs of people who were comfortable in each other's company despite having a shared brush with death the night before.

"We were talking about taking a few days off and visiting Oxford. Henry and his wife have a cottage up there on their property, plus rooms in the main house," Morgan said.

"And you want me to join you," Skelter said. "While you guys are locked in your room like a pair of newlyweds? Not friggen likely, but I would like to get in on questioning these guys and then get home to my family."

"Can we get in on the interrogation?" Platt said, his eyes gleaming and all signs of fatigue gone from his face. "I though the local cops or MI6 would be handling most of that."

"You just want to torture these guys, Platt, admit it," Morgan chuckled as the elevator arrived.

Platt smiled, "Of course I do! Can I have it all? Can we get that out of the way, and then go to Oxford?"

"You're like a little kid," Morgan said with a grin. "You remind me of when I was all new at this and everything was laced in intrigue and suspense."

"Are you saying that changes?" asked Skelter as they stepped off the elevator and walked toward the dining room.

"Not at all," Morgan said. "Although I have a feeling you might be observing rather than in on the interrogation, you probably should both be here for it. Let's plan for Oxford by the end of the week. If it works, fuck it, we go, and if some other arsepicks need fixing, we'll get on with that instead."

Morgan looked at the young hostess standing at the podium on the edge of the hotel café. The young woman's eyes were wide. Her ponytail of long box lightened hair bobbed up and down as she struggled to comes to terms with the attractive Morgan and her wayward mouth.

Morgan looked at the hostess and said sweetly, "Three for breakfast, please."

Chapter Eleven

The wayward Ambassador was located at the Chinese embassy the day after the incident at Steeves' home. He managed to avoid getting arrested immediately, but the Foreign and Commonwealth Office quickly weighed in on the matter and refused to extend diplomatic immunity to him, since the charges were serious. He was denied exit from Britain and picked up trying to get on a plane at Gatwick airport. It didn't take long for ACTI to connect him to Meriweather, thanks to James' efficient work and the prevalence of CCTV footage in London. The files showed the two of them meeting on a couple of occasions, and equally as damaging for Meriweather, were more meetings between her and additional members of the Chinese consulate.

"We've got good proof that the Ambassador was behind the attack on Steeves' home, but still only circumstantial evidence of the Chinese being responsible for *Joy19*," Morgan said. She was closeted in her office with Steeves, Skelter, Dr. Bendar, Platt, James, and Natalie. With the weekend approaching, it was time for Skelter to head back to New York, and the trip to Oxford for Morgan and Platt. "Evidence that *Joy19* came out of China is well supported by investigations gathered, although we still need to be cautious throwing all our eggs in one basket. There is still an exceptional likelihood someone based in the U.S. or with significant interest in the U.S. is involved, and even directing the operation to some degree. Dr. Bendar, do you have any thoughts? Since you're new here and still have the benefit of looking from the outside, I'd like to hear your ideas."

"From the evidence I've seen, it's possible that a large organization was behind the initial release from China. Some of the evidence points to organized crime, partly because it's drugs, and partly because it's a huge initiative, but even that has to have a root somewhere. We are still looking through the data, which continues to update regularly. The next stage includes finding out if the money funding organized crime is from other criminal enterprises, or what seems equally likely, from one or more political influences," Dr. Bendar paused and looked at the group.

"Just a sec," Platt said, sitting up sharply as the information sunk in. "You're saying there's proof now that someone inside the U.S. is funding the manufacture and distribution of drugs inside of China."

"Possibly," Dr. Bendar said. "It wouldn't be the first time someone in a political position had big plans and paid organized crime to execute those plans, but we still don't know all the intricacies for sure."

"Maybe we could start exercising some pressure to get faster answers by diving into organized crime in the U.S.," Morgan said looking at Skelter.

"You mean by arresting and questioning members of organized crime?" Dr. Bendar asked.

Morgan shook her head. "No, not yet, or we will tip them off. My first steps are to do some serious cyber and phone stalking, as well as using video surveillance. Let's get James and Natalie to see what they can find out. There's got to be more to this, and I want quick answers, so we don't risk having to release the Chinese ambassador, nor Meriweather. If needed, we can bring The Fellas back in. Skelter, I'll ask you to do some gentle work with the FBI and DEA to see if they could have anything that can help us."

Skelter looked at Platt and asked, "Rob, what's the chances that a soldier coming back from a deployment could get hired to bring drugs back with them?"

"Depending on where they've been and whether they fly back on a military flight or a commercial one, it's possible," Platt said thoughtfully. "When I was on my first tour of Afghanistan, people pushed drugs at us all the time. Afghani citizens would try to put them in your hand. Children, women. But we don't have soldiers coming back from China...although we've been in Kazakhstan and Afghanistan during the past year, so it's conceivable that the Chinese could be working on a roundabout way of tagging returning soldiers, but I think it's unlikely. There's not a lot of tolerance for that kind of thing in the military. Don't get me wrong, there are drug problems, but not many soldiers would want to be drug dealers for someone they meet while on military business."

"Who else do we know of that has lots of people moving between the U.S. and China?" Morgan asked. "Let's figure this out."

"There are about 350,000 students from China studying at U.S. universities and colleges," Dr. Bendar said looking up from her tablet. "That's a huge number of potential distributors, traffickers, or mules. There are certainly far more students than there are military returning from deployments, and they are easy to access if we follow through the dry cleaners. Some of those students enter the U.S. or wherever they are studying more than once a year if they go home for summer, term breaks, or Christmas," she said. She pursed her lips thoughtfully.

"There is some interesting information about China and the U.S. business scene, too," Natalie said. "Do you want to hear this now, or shall I send it to you in an email?"

"Let us have it, Nat. Sounds timely," Morgan said, nodding to the young woman.

"Well, China has been at odds with the U.S. over trade for months now, but it's not because of reasons people may think. In the news we hear the leaders of both countries trading declarations of tariffs, and threatening arrests, and so on. But the Chinese have a very different approach to business than we do. They are a communist country, and so their business policy tends to be made in favor of Chinese companies, and they do things like develop policy before they consider foreign investment, for example. Countries like the U.S. like bottom up policies, which they feel fosters more room to be innovative, profit generating, and works well in America's capitalist system. China has an initiative for economic growth called *Made in China 2025*, and it's especially related to tech. They are okay with achieving growth in the Chinese economy at the expense of international competition. They have also invested extensively in other markets around the globe to get money flowing into China. They share the number one spot as a world powerhouse economy with the United States, but they don't think they need more U.S. cooperation to continue to grow."

"So it's conceivable that the Chinese don't give a shit about what happens anywhere, just so long as they get what they need," Skelter said, not asking a direct question but wanting his point clarified.

"Yes, that's correct," said Natalie.

"So if China is intent on disrupting the U.S. market and using drugs to do it, what's the chances they care about spin off damage to all these other countries – Canada, Europe, Russia – where *Joy19* is showing up?" Steeves asked quietly.

"They won't. It's collateral damage," said Morgan with a sigh. "And so whomever or whatever is sending the money to China to launch the *Joy19* problem is in this up to their necks. And potentially the Chinese are utilizing students as a delivery system."

James said quietly, "I've just had a terrible thought..."

Morgan nodded at him, "Go on."

James looked at the ceiling momentarily, and then said in a rush, "What's the chances that the Chinese are getting money for this effort and they have recruited organized crime as a distribution system...they'd have to control a huge crime syndicate, nothing puny...and the Chinese have manipulated the drug rings into thinking each syndicate will control the drug trade, but at some point, like when

China achieves their China 2025 plan...then China's next steps include calling all the debt they have bankrolled for other countries. As those economies fail, they fall under Chinese control. With the launch of *Joy19* focussed mainly in America, it's likely that an American entity is paying the Chinese to create and distribute a drug that won't just take down the U.S. economy, but also several related economies...a move that will ultimately benefit China."

There was a long pause, and Morgan could hear the blood pumping in her ears. "James and Natalie...be very careful with the data you have and look deeper at that. Call Henry and get him to help with what you need to create additional data sets. Be extremely diligent to maintain data integrity. If what you posit is true, and we're going to prove it, then we have to know that your theory isn't warping the data to prove your hypothesis. See what the data supports."

Morgan stood to end the meeting, nodding to everyone as they filed out the door. Platt remained.

"Sounds like a working weekend, hey?" he said.

"I'm sorry about that, but it might be," Morgan said smiling sheepishly. "We'll take a chopper ride up to Oxford if you are okay with that."

"I thought you didn't like riding in helicopters?" Platt said with raised eyebrows.

"It'll add some excitement to your visit. Besides, driving up there on a Friday night there will be a ton of traffic, and then we'll both be wishing we had stayed in London. Henry or his chef will pick us up at a small airfield not far from his place. That way, we also have a fast way back here if all hell breaks loose," she said.

"Are you expecting all hell to break loose?" Platt asked.

"Always Rob."

He moved toward her and circled her in his arms. "You're wearing your handgun in the office I see."

"Yeah, I usually have it on me. I like to be at the ready for any crap coming at us." She tipped up her face and kissed him on the lips. "Isn't it fun hanging out with me?"

"I wouldn't have it any other way," he said, kissing her back.

End Notes

I'm grateful you have read this book, and I hope you enjoyed it! There is nothing quite so satisfying for an author to do than create books that readers want.

I spent six years in the Canadian Armed Forces, then went on to work as a teacher, career counsellor, writer, and instructional designer. Having had a variety of jobs, and with the privilege of living across the country, I try to draw from those experiences and the amazing people I've met to give depth to my writing. I enjoy turning random thoughts and unnerving dreams into stories, and it was a couple of dreams plus some head down intensive research that led me to create Morgan Winfeld's stories.

My work has been published in collections of short stories, magazines, textbooks, some ghost writing, and more. The first assignment to get me excited about writing came from my sixth-grade teacher, Mr. Burrows. He asked me to ghost write a story that started me down a path of researching, reading, and eventually gathering an admirable collection of rejection emails.

This book is the second novella about Morgan Winfeld. If you'd like to learn what's coming up next, I hope you'll keep in touch, and connect online. It would mean a lot to me if you could leave a review on Amazon, Goodreads, Kobo, or wherever you like to find reviews that encourage you to read good books.

Facebook PamRWriter
Instagram @PamDRobertson
Twitter @PamRobertson
Web pamrobertson.org

64279266R00090

Made in the USA
Middletown, DE
28 August 2019